The First Of
The Assassination Diaries

The Bishop

Copyright © Maddy 2013

Maddy asserts moral right to be identified as the author of this work

All rights reserved.

No part of this E-book publication may be reproduced, stored in any retrieval
system or transmitted in any form or by any means, electronic, mechanical, photocopying, recording without the written permission of the publisher, nor otherwise circulated in any form of binding or cover other than which it is published and without a similar condition including this condition being imposed on the subsequent purchaser.

First published as an E-book in the United Kingdom by Next Century Books April 2013

Cover Design and Layout by Steve Hanlon

Paperback Edition
Printed and bound in the UK by Biddles
Part of The MPG Print Group

ISBN 978-0-9572396-7-8

The Author

The Assassin aka "Maddy"

Assassination is the extreme form of censorship

George Bernard Shaw – 'The Rejected Statement

The Three Assassination Diaries So Far Received

The First Assassination Diary – The Bishop
The Second Assassination Diary – The Mandarin
The Third Assassination Diary – The Oligarch

More Diaries Are Promised

Discovery of The Assassination Diaries

A secluded house among trees on the outskirts of a small town caught fire one morning and exploded.
Totally destroyed, the property resisted attempts by the fire service and other authorities to find a cause. Nor did they find evidence of bodies or much sign of anyone recently living in the house.
The owner, a woman of indeterminate age, had not been seen for several months before the explosion. Being an author of travel books, this did not seem unusual as she left the house empty for varying periods from a few weeks to six months or more. Although she took part in the general life of the town, not one of the townspeople appeared to know her well, or, indeed know anything about her background and origins.
A search of the premises by the authorities discovered a fireproof strong box containing only a number of bound documents that turned out to be a series of Diaries.

Prologue

For this Diary I'll use the name Madeleine – Maddy for short.

I'm small and pretty, with long blonde hair, a great figure and I'm a contract killer.

You can't properly call a woman hit-man. Nor can you say hit-woman or hit-girl or, even more classy, hit-lady. So I prefer the term Assassin. When selected to this calling I gave my life to it as a nun does to religion.

I entered University with two languages and came out with six, along with two top degrees and – as with all young people – a need to change the world.

The chance came when, recruited within days of leaving, I agreed to an interview in an expensive house on the edge of town. Stunned by the rich opulence of the place I hardly heard the opening words of my Recruiter.

'We saw your potential in finishing school and followed your progress ever since. In University you collected four more languages, two great degrees and excelled at sport. You avoided alcohol and drugs, played every possible sport and took on and beat men in martial arts. Your father showed you how to handle guns before the age of ten and you became a superb shot. You have everything we need and if you agree you will become rich in your own right but give up what is seen as a normal life.'

He explained the job in detail and said, 'Think before you agree. To say yes means you'll act out a lonely life in the shadows.'

I still said 'Yes'. Why shouldn't I? My whole lonely life so far had been an act. Adding shadows would make no difference. And I found the thought of killing people who deserve to die quite attractive.

They sent me straight to wilds of another country for three years detailed training in two more martial arts, three more languages and many ways to kill.

My training included tracking and killing Targets in towns, villages, mountains, ravines, deserts and seas and skills in escaping after a Hit from those towns and villages and over those mountains, ravines, deserts and seas, with or without equipment.

It included the art of disguise and fading into the background in any crowd, city or situation before or after a Hit.

It included the stripping, maintaining and shooting every possible weapon an Assassin might use.

It included burglary, lock-breaking, safe-breaking, the disabling of security systems, the elimination of armed guards by knife, bare hands or silenced pistol.

It included killing Targets in a dozen different ways, using knives, handguns, sniping rifles, poisons and chemicals or, again, bare hands.

And it included detailed training in many kinds and styles of sex. Lots and lots of sex.

I enjoyed every moment of the whole course, but most of all I enjoyed the sex. Instructors, both male and female, showed me how to seduce using Thai, Chinese, Japanese, Swedish and American techniques. American? Yes. They lead the way in some really interesting ideas.

And Indian sex. 'Not that too vague and time consuming tantric rubbish. Stick to the stuff on temple walls. You'll need to stay fit and supple but I'm sure you'll handle that.'

Before release at the end of the course I asked, 'Have you turned me into a psychopath?'

'No,' said my Recruiter. 'We've enhanced what you already had. Not many get even halfway through. You've passed with flying colours. Now go into the world and await your first instruction.'

Final advice from Recruiter: 'Go to where you don't know the language. Learn it and never use it outside that country so no-one can ever trace you home, including us. Who knows? The day may come when we need to eliminate you.'

Chapter 1

I flew to another continent and disappeared into a secret life. Not even my Handler knew where I settled.

A small town I chose deep in an area of great forest seemed perfect. The nearest airport over two hundred miles away meant no tourists. The local people and their own inbred entertainment made any stranger stand out for examination and discussion.

I took a new name and a small house among trees on the outskirts, telling the few people I managed to speak with, 'I write travel books and need peace to concentrate when back from my research around the world.'

Of course, this helped explain my planned absences for any length of time. On final briefing, Handler told me, 'Depending on the Target and the difficulty of approach, a contracted Hit can take anything from a couple of weeks to six months or more.'

The locals became used to me and I began to pick up the language, collecting at first a few words, then a few sentences and, after six months, basic grammar and fair fluency.

Handler promised I would be left alone for at least six months to allow my credibility to build. So I spent that time getting to know my neighbours and the townspeople by joining in on everything I could; national days, local fairs and charity functions. I even became a supporter of the local sports teams, cheering them on and leaping with glee when they scored, although I knew few rules of their games.

I also wrote the travel book I researched in the time before I came to their town. I knew little of the subject or country I had "researched" but the book seemed good enough to publish. So I flew to another country, found an agent and within weeks three publishers were raving over the manuscript.

Now, with my cover established, I could relax and find some sex. A vibrator is fun but no good at foreplay so I took a lover in my forest town – a hunky local worker – and taught him a few new tricks on how to give and receive pleasure.

I found money no problem. Every month a great wodge of cash crashed into my main numbered bank account in a small tax-dodging country. Most stayed there earning interest, but a reasonable monthly "salary" arrived in my local account, having taken a dizzying bank-to-bank route round the world. Eventually I could expect a reasonable amount of travel book royalties to deepen my cover.

So I sat back and enjoyed a restful and pleasant way of life for seven months until one day my anonymous Cloud Mail-Box pinged with its first coded message.

Go to the Cote d'Azure and await instructions.

Chapter 2

I travelled to the South of France and found a pleasant hill-village behind Nice.

I rented an apartment and, with nothing else but to wait for instructions on my Target, I began research on the many specialist brothels that abound to serve the rich and famous of Europe.

This became a joy and distraction – or so I thought – until my Cloud Mail-Box pinged with the instruction: *Find and eliminate The Bishop.*

I set aside my brothel book and started researching churches and cathedrals and bishops. I found a bishop in Nice, an Archbishop in Marseilles and one Russian Orthodox bishop in a fancy church in Nice.

At the Orthodox Church I heard of a bishop investigated for diddling behind the altar with an eleven-year old boy but that had been years ago, so he couldn't be my target.

A pity. I'd love to pop a queer priest.

So I went back to my extremely pleasant brothels research, wondering all the time: *Who or what is The Bishop. And how do I find him?*

I sent a question via my Cloud Mail-Box and received an immediate reply: *Look in the sewers.*

The sewers?

From this cryptic reply I realised that this first mission is a test of my ability to act alone in tracking and securing a Target. I decided there and then never again to ask for help.

"The Sewers" means a criminal, not a priest. I thought hard and deep for several days on a plan to single out a criminal on a coast riddled with crime, without finding an answer. Then came a stroke of luck.

Sitting at a pavement cafe sipping some local concoction, my eye caught a glaring red headline in an abandoned newspaper on the next table. I reached out and grabbed before the breeze carried it away.

Smoothing the page on my table I read the big banner in mounting excitement.

THE BISHOP WINS AGAIN

A quick scan of the article made my heart leap.

Here is my breakthrough. Here is my man. In print. And with a picture.

I took a deep calming breath and a sip at my concoction before reading again, this time slowly and with concentration. The article and picture, both short on detail, gave me enough to start tracking my Target.

A column of words in breathless tabloid-ese, told how this man; well-known to the authorities as a MASTER CRIMINAL – had AGAIN cheated justice. It rushed on, piling cliché and cliché onto cliché, that this RUTHLESS GANGSTER and his HENCHMEN lived a life of untouchable ease and luxury on their ILL-GOTTEN-GAINS from drugs, prostitution, arms smuggling, gambling, murder, along the Coast and in all the large cities, Paris, Lyon, Bordeaux...

The article went big on his luxury houses and luxury yacht and luxury brothels and luxury women. In fact it went big on the word luxury. But it didn't say where he lived.

The colour picture seemed almost as useless. It showed a crowd of big men surrounding a small man obviously hurrying from the courthouse. Snapped over shoulders and through a forest of heads, the picture showed only raised arm of the man who must be The Bishop – expensive watch glinting gold in a shard of sunlight – and an ear partly covered by strands of black hair.

Not much.

But a start.

I took the paper straight to the best brothel I knew and whispered 'Where do I find him?' to my favourite lover just as she reached orgasm. She froze and hissed, 'He owns this place but he's dangerous. He kills women he doesn't like. Stay away.'

'I can't. I need him for my book.'

'You'll never get near to him. But if he hear's you're searching he'll find you. '

Although I tried again to make her come, I'd spoiled her big moment and she told the Madame and got me thrown out. I missed her because she was a wild one, well worth the extra money.

This incident worried me. Had I broken cover? Would The Bishop come after me?

I knew I must move. I abandoned my lovely hill-village, went down to Nice and disappeared into the cover of two new characters.

Chapter 3

I left everything in the hill-village apartment except my leather yoga mat and brothels manuscript. Brothel writing is more fun than travel writing, with plenty of action and free luxury sex along the way. No point in being a writer and not enjoying what you do.

In Nice, I hid for two weeks in a tiny hotel room working on the identities to take up as cover in this new place, sliding out only to eat in cheap cafes and buy a few low grade anonymous clothes.

On these hurried trips through mean streets of this poorest area of the city I decided on two characters so different no-one would make connections if searching for me. I decided to get the hard bit over first, so for the first phase of my hunt, became Dominique St Jean, a downtrodden drudge.

Apart from perhaps using her on odd occasions I left my other more comfortable character, Eleanor Aquitaine, for the second phase; the closing phase; the killing phase.

Dominique will do the work and prepare the ground from shadows and twilight.

Eleanor will get the glory as star of a shocking drama with great publicity, although never able to take the limelight or show up for the award.

Eleanor, when used, will pass for a beautiful high society whore; rich lady of leisure; screen goddess or millionaire's wife, as I choose from time to time and act to act.

Oh, this is the woman I looked forward to being as I prepared to be Dominique.

Chapter 4

I moved to a small, dirty lodging house and became Dominique. Poor helpless woman, so similar to many of those I observed trudging these pavements between low-grade job and rat infested apartment block. She allowed me to drop further from sight as a shadow among shadows, without nosey hotel owners checking my comings and goings.

After cutting Dominique's hair into stringy lumps and dyeing it patchy black I removed all makeup and bought the lowest quality clothes imaginable. I must admit, seeing this pale ugly thing in mirrors and shop window reflections plunged me into depression, but, following my detailed training, I made Dominique almost impossible to memorise.

I began to feel safe.

It took me no time to find work as kitchen maid in a rough Arab cafe down a stinking lane. The owner – a fat greasy Moroccan with a heart of gold – thrust a large plate of couscous before me and said, 'For the sake of Allah, sit and eat *habibi*. You look closer to death than a sheep for slaughter.'

He took me in as a daughter and, whilst making sure I worked without cease, paid me well and tried to fatten me up, laughing and telling me, 'If only you were Muslim and plump I'd marry you to one of my sons.'

Washing filthy plates in hot water and scrubbing floors and tables soon roughened and reddened my poor hands. Starting early and finishing late I returned exhausted to my apartment, barely bigger than a cupboard. During lonely evenings I sat staring at the wall, wishing I could be Eleanor.

But until that happy day I must use Dominique's time to the full and avoid boredom, I started a travel book about the slums and cafes and people of this terrible deprived rich-city suburb. Living the nightmare made for easier writing.

I found it impossible to remain depressed in the noisy, happy cafe. Customers of all sorts laughed, drank, held shouted conversations in Arabic and French and swapped lecherous gossip.

I picked up the rough local accent in both languages by listening and speaking and soon could pass myself off as a child of the *bidonvilles*. I learned coarse phrases from criminals, con-men, illegal immigrants batting back their lewd suggestions with humour in their own slang to great laughter and more ribaldry. And I began to pick up snatches of gossip about crime and criminals, a word here; a hint there.

Clearing tables late one evening I heard a comment on the blaring television screwed and chained to the wall about two young people washed onto the beach by high winds.

'It's The Bishop,' grunted a drunken pickpocket.

My heart thumped.

'A bishop drowned?' I asked.

'Not *A* Bishop, habibi, *The* Bishop. It's The Bishop who'll have made those young people drown. She'll be one of his girlfriends or one of his whores. He'll be her piece on the side. Probably one of The Bishop's gorillas caught at it when he shouldn't be at it.'

'Shut up or you'll be in the water too,' someone hissed.

Next morning I bought a newspaper. Not drowned. Both shot in the head. The man missing his balls. The woman missing both breasts. The paper hinted at The Bishop with a picture of a large house by the sea and a fancy yacht.

My second break.

I sent a coded message through my Cloud-**B**ox
Target sighted. The hunt is on.

Chapter 5

Now with something to go on I began a trawl of restaurants and bars every second night, hunting for gossip or clues.

At first I heard plenty of gossip, but, eventually, only one clue – The Bishop's gorillas are known as Chessmen.

No one told me. I heard it whispered when a large overdressed young man strode into a bar and two drunken men, clinging to the rail for support, nodded in his direction and whispered.

I leaned over and said, 'Did you say he plays chess?'

My nearest drunk put a finger to his lips and hissed, 'Shsss.'

The other tapped the side of his nose and, his tongue addled by alcohol, murmured, 'He's one of The Bishop's.'

I leaned forward and said, 'Who's?'

'Shut up,' said Drunk One.

'Let's go,' said Drunk Two.

They released their grip on the rail – just about their only point of balance – and, holding each other upright, shuffled uncertainly from the bar without looking back.

The Chessmen? So this is a Chessman?

I studied his arrogant confidence; his expensive dark suit; his black slicked hair; the way he snapped his fingers for immediate and servile attention. You'll have seen his style hundreds of times in French and American films.

He even had a ridiculous little pencil-line moustache. Thin black and neat it ran across under his nose; most certainly tended and primped and preened by some luxury *coiffeuse* along the Boulevard.

So this is a Chessman. Can he lead me anywhere? Should follow him? Should I leave now and keep coming back to this bar night after night? He may be a regular here with other Chessmen. Perhaps he'll even bring The Bishop?

Unlikely. The man in the newspaper picture would never be seen in this place or any like it.

Decision made.

Follow.

He called for a bill. Nodded at the dismissive hand-wave that said, 'Not for you.'

Accepting one last free drink he sat back, hair pomade gleaming. His eyes swept the bar, studying every woman but me. Never gave me a glance.

Quite right. What sensible man would bother with this skinny, mousy little thing?

His gaze didn't even pause.

Good. I'm invisible.

I slipped out and disappeared into the shadowed palm trees along the beach, fingers crossed that he would walk, not drive.

He stepped onto the Boulevard and marched off through the late-evening crowd. I followed to the nearest casino. He trotted up the steps and in the door between bowing and saluting doormen.

Hoping he may be a regular along with The Bishop I watched from my palm trees lair every second night for two weeks.

Using a small pair of binoculars I studied every man entering and leaving the casino and saw him twice, but always alone.

Chapter 6

Both times he left the casino and jumped into a waiting car. I couldn't follow so stole a small motor-bike for the next sighting.

He is not my prey. He is my only lead. He is my tethered goat. My route to The Bishop. I must not lose him.

So I remained patient in the night shadows.

Fat Greasy Moroccan and his customers teased me for disappearing every other night on my bike. 'You have a lover,' they cried. 'He is a lucky man and you a lucky woman getting cock so often. Not even the beautiful ones get so much. You must be great performer'.

They are right. I am a great performer and my patience paid off. At the end of my second week, a third sighting; my Chessman strolling down the Boulevard holding hands with a large fat Arab.

Through binoculars I studied Arab from head to toe. Wearing an expensive dish-dash, hands laden with gold and diamonds sparkling in the kaleidoscope neon lights; he looked every inch the rich mark or criminal. Which?

With round unshaven face and tiny eyes constantly scanning the crowded pavement I decided; *Criminal*.

My second tethered goat. A second lead to The Bishop. Tonight I must follow one or both and find a house or home or criminal base.

They nearly caught me out by leaving the casino after only thirty minutes, hurrying down the steps and into a large white car. I scampered to my bike and whizzed after them, swerving through the traffic until I picked them up a hundred metres ahead and settled back to follow, turning north away from the sea and the Boulevard.

The car drove at slow pace through increasingly dense traffic to a large shining football stadium surrounded by a great throng pushing in through small gates. Chessman and Arab left the car and shoved through the crowd to a special door that opened the moment they arrived.

Another wait – almost two hours – before the door opened and they came out. I spent the time checking where their car parked and wandering round the stadium with several thousand fans obviously without tickets but wanting to be part of the noisy glory.

From the excitement when the game ended and the crowd thrust out it seemed their team won. With thousands of excited fans pushing past I had trouble staying in position to watch the special door but eventually it opened and my two Marks came out, slapping backs and shaking hands with half a dozen other large, flashy men.

My two started off towards the car. I tried to follow a short way behind but an eddy in the crowd carried me in a half circle against Arab's heavy stomach. I bounced off and came face-to-face with Chessman. He looked down and laughed but a second look brought a frown.

Did he recognise me from the cafe? Did I see suspicion in his eyes? I dived into the crowd and watched from an angle. He certainly stopped laughing and murmured in Arab's ear.

I turned away and became part of the crowd, walking down the road towards Nice town centre. Glancing over my shoulder I saw the fancy white car pull out and drive the opposite way.

But Arab had not gone. He had joined the crowd to stride after me, his eyes fixed to make sure I did not disappear.

Chapter 7

I skipped along, looking over my shoulder as though nervous at this obvious pursuit.

He took the bait and made sure he kept up with long strides. The crowd thinned and I saw him tiring and beginning to puff. So I slowed allowing him to rest and catch up.

Eventually we were almost alone by an unlit lane and he spurted, grabbed me round the waist and dragged me into the shadow.

'What do you want?' I bleated, struggling and kicking, acting the frightened young woman.

Hissing into my ear he snarled, 'First I'm going to fuck you, then you'll answer some questions and then I may kill you.'

He turned me round and banged me against the wall. Holding a forearm across my throat he punched my face. My head snapped back against the bricks and I began to feel angry. He hauled up my skirt and with a knee forced my legs apart. His hand slid down to rip away my thong and slap against my quim.

An electric flash of pleasure raced through my body. The combination of punch, anger and rough hand exploring my vitals made me almost surrender to a bit of rough sex. I wriggled and thrust against his hand, enjoying the sensation.

'Keep still,' he growled and made to push me to the ground.

But the fool had left my arms free so with clenched forefinger knuckle I whipped a Kyusho nerve strike at a point just below his left ear. All feeling gone he flopped to the ground in an untidy heap.

As he fell I held his head. A cracked skull would be useless to me.

I knelt close and whispered, 'I think I'm better at this than you,' straightening his arms and legs. 'There. Now you're comfortable we can talk.'

Still conscious he stared up, shock and fear in his eyes.

'Who are you?' he whispered.

'Doesn't matter. Who is your friend? Tell me his name or I'll hurt you'

'I don't know his name.'

Tightening my thumb and forefinger on his throat nerves, I whispered, 'Try and remember.'

'Chessmen never tell their name.'

Sounds reasonable. I wouldn't either.

'Where does he live?'

'I don't know.'

'Where is his favourite restaurant?'

He gave me the name of a top eating place along The Boulevard.

'Does The Bishop go there too?'

'Is that who you're after?'

'Where does The Bishop live?'

He summoned enough energy to launch a gob of spit at me so I finished him off with a finger pinch to the windpipe, feeling satisfaction at the way his eyes rolled and glazed towards death.

I took his wallet, pulled the rings from his hands and collected a large gold medallion chain from round his neck.

This makes it easy for police to report a robbery and close a case, though cause of death will puzzle the coroner.

They'll probably know who he is but I doubt many will mourn his passing.

The bike I torched on a secluded beach. No fingerprints. No forensics. All safe.

One down, how many to go?

Chapter 8

I rode the bus back to the cafe where Fat Greasy Moroccan and his customers laughed and teased for the cut and bruise on my face.

'Didn't give him enough?' they howled in derision. 'Shirking on the job? Did his wife catch you at it?'

I hung my head and tried to hide, giving a good act of being embarrassed and contrite because, on the bus, I decided that now is the time to leave and take up a new identity.

Next morning I told Fat Greasy Moroccan that my lover's wife sent two men to beat him up and they included me but I'd managed to run away.

'Who are they?' he growled. 'I'll send my sons to smash them.'

'No. That will only make things worse. I must leave for a while but I'll be back.'

'You are welcome any time, *habibi*. You are my beloved daughter.'

He paid me off and avoiding a big hug I went to my apartment to prepare for departure the next morning. Fresh from a good sleep I paid my final rent, bought a morning paper and took a bus along the coast to a new town by the sea.

Passing a small rocky cove I saw my torched motorbike lying in the sand, black and purple from petrol flames. Such an ugly sight - how it spoiled that beautiful beach.

But it seems the police had not connected it to the murdered Arab I read about in my paper, written in the usual gasping-with-excitement tabloid red banner headlined article.

GANGLAND SLAYING

Well known Arab criminal found dead in alley. Director of casinos group suspected connected to MASTER CRIMINAL known as THE BISHOP found MYSTERIOUSLY DEAD in alley. Wallet and jewellery missing believed stolen but police working on theory this is a trick to lead them away from an obvious GANGLAND HIT probably the result of internal feuding...etc, etc.

So, there I have it. The police think the death is a gangland hit but The Bishop knows it is not. Chessman will remember me and thinks he will recognise me when next we meet.

So he and The Bishop will be looking for me.

Good.

This brings them out of their shadows and into mine. I'll still be invisible but they'll be in the open. My tethered goat worked. At first they'll send the goons, the foot soldiers. I'll deal with them then start working my way up the ladder towards The Bishop.

But for the moment I need to disappear and regroup.

Skipping from bus to rail and back to bus I moved a hundred kilometres along the coast until I found a town large enough to suit the next part of my plan.

For privacy I again rented a small flat but this time in a middle-class area. A few days on the beach healed my bruise and removed the deliberate grey pallor of poor, dowdy, kitchen worker Dominique. I went shopping for clothes to be worn by a quiet, intellectual travel writer researching the history of artists and art galleries in Provence.

And I bought an expensive blonde wig to cover and allow my hair to grow and start turning back to natural blonde. After a couple of months I travelled inland to visit art galleries and have my natural hair properly cut and styled.

I know that Handler will hear news of the strange unsolved murder in Nice and work out from the manner of death that I am in the hunting phase.

He will not contact me or I him. But we both know more death must follow before I strike Target, no matter how long it takes.

I stayed four months on the coast before moving to Paris for the next stage of my operation

Chapter 9

The quiet, intellectual, unglamorous travel writer in her cheap middle-class dress avoided Nice and its airport and travelled high-speed train first class from Avignon.

I kept close watch on the afternoon passengers in my carriage. Not one of the travelling businessmen bothered to give me more than a passing glance and their expensively dressed women ignored me completely. No competition from this little mouse.

Now that Dominique is, for the time being, tucked away in the cupboard, I concentrated on a new identity for Paris and perhaps beyond.

The beautiful Eleanor is not yet ready to bring out so I decided to become Simone Dubois, a well-off young woman and budding travel writer from the provinces looking for a good time in the big city.

I found a small, comfortable, expensive hotel among the lanes and alleys around the Champs Elysees and went shopping for Simone's stylish new outfits, then – dressed to impress – entered two of the biggest banks in France and opened an account in each, one as Simone for immediate use and one as Eleanor for later.

Both bank managers found charm and fascination in my beautiful clothes – a peep of breast and hint of thigh – and Simone' slightly rough South-of-France accent with its earthy appeal and the elegant educated Eleanor. They made light of the rules, accepting my bogus proof of identity with almost identical shrugs.

Both asked me out to dinner and I accepted, 'But not now Monsieur. I shall contact you.'

I left each bank with a business card and a hint of sexual promise in my handshake. A day later I probably surprised and delighted my new friends by transferring a quarter of a million dollars into each account. It is wonderful what you can achieve by showing a bit of tit and a large amount of money.

Then I reverted to Simone the travel writer and started work studying Paris.

I spent two weeks on the standard tourist trail, to keep my agent and travel-publisher happy then, bored to tears, dived with relish into the disgusting sewer of brothels and private sex life of this city.

Chapter 10

The city of Paris felt big and aggressive after the gentle airs of Provence, with large, flashy brothels designed to cover every taste and deviation.

They were also very expensive so after a couple of paid visits and some quite exciting lesbian encounters I changed sides and joined two high-class brothels and one top rate call-girl outfit.

Working as a quality prostitute allowed meetings with rich and powerful men. I enjoyed plenty of male sex, at the same time drawing in lots of cash.

After exhausting my lovers in deliberately over-active sex sessions I dropped questioning hints on The Bishop's organisation in Paris, if it existed. Most knew only the name but one powerful politician with the oddest of sexual tastes, asked me, while gasping for breath, 'Why are you interested?'

'I'm fascinated by crime.'

'That's because you live in the countryside,' he said. 'You don't want to ask too many questions about this man. I know him. I've met him. He's dangerous. Stay away from such subjects and enjoy Paris while you can. Before you go home, try a couple of our private sex clubs – you won't need to work so hard and you'll meet and see some exciting people. With your disgusting skills you'll be a perfect fit for that scene.'

Before leaving he scribbled a couple of addresses. 'These are two of the best. You'll meet plenty of people and enjoy all sorts of things that even you would never have thought of.'

I rested for a week – successful prostitution can be quite exhausting – and returned to being a rich but uncultured tourist. I called both bankers for dinner dates and enjoyed two entirely different evenings.

Banker One – sweet, gentle, good natured and nervous – I met in a small restaurant alongside the Seine. He lived with his elderly mother in an expensive suburb, 'She's quite old and I look after her, so have very little social life. This is a wonderful experience for me.'

When I asked, he professed no knowledge of The Bishop at first, then, whispering, admitted his bank held some criminal enterprise accounts. He had the same question, 'Why do you ask?'

I gave the same answer, 'I'm fascinated by crime.'

After a little sweet talk persuasion, he agreed, 'To help in research for the crime book you are writing. I'll check secretly through some of the accounts, although it's illegal, you understand,'

After dinner I took Banker One down by the river. We sat on a seat in the moonlight and I allowed him a fumble then gave him a quick pull, much to his delight. I don't think the poor innocent had ever come across anything like it until he came over my thigh with a muted howl and a shudder.

I decided not to become too involved with Banker One as if he learned or guessed too much about me I may have to kill him. And that would be awful for his poor mother.

Banker Two turned out to be a different kettle of fish. Paris born and bred, he spent the whole evening with his hand under the table, trying to get up my skirt and into my thong. I finally allowed it during dessert, wriggling against his finger and enjoying the sensation of knowing that curious diners watched from the other side of the room.

Before he jumped me in his flat I told him over coffee of my small son and jealous husband on our farm in Provence. It made no difference. He tore off my clothes and spent an hour going at me from every angle. I must say his is the most active French cock I'd experienced up to that date, so, in return, I pleasured him several times in ways he had never before met.

'My God, we must do this again,' he groaned, finally collapsing under the weight of continual effort.

'Only if you can get me some information,' I said and took the risk of asking specific questions about The Bishop, telling him, 'I am really a private investigator working for his wife. But you must be careful. I understand this criminal is especially dangerous.'

He sat up with a tough-man sneer on his face. 'Do you think I'm frightened of a stinking low-life criminal? I'm far too clever to be caught by such a man. We have several of his criminal gang accounts, and accounts for his wife three of his mistresses. Give me a few days. I'll dig out some details. We can meet for another wonderful evening and, depending how good you are to me I'll give you plenty of dirt.'

What a stupid man.

I won't need to kill him.

He'll certainly arrange that for himself.

Chapter 11

The first private sex club I visited opened my eyes to a world I never imagined.

A large, rambling cellar in mid Paris filled with perhaps five-hundred people wandering through red-lit rooms and corridors could have been an artist's vision of hell, without actual flames.

Not that this satanic place needed flames. Skin hugging leather trousers, bulging jockstraps glistening with jewels, cut out bras, painted breasts, dangling cocks, women naked except for long leather boots; all flickering in flashing red strobes that showed the feeling, fondling, fucking in every corner of the cellar and every nook and cranny of the many bodies rubbing each other in pleasure.

A tiny young woman strolled by, naked from necklace to glittering waist belt wandered past, perfect breasts rolling in time to her delicate walk. Her long skirt, split into swirling panels, showed nothing underneath but a tantalising glimpse of her tight little bush.

I fought an urge to follow for a feel and play with those amazing tits, so delicious and available, but decided not to become involved with women tonight. I am here in this place for the men.

I came to a dance floor crowded with couples pleasuring each other to music. I pushed through, copping a few feels of my own as I passed by. I stopped to watch a beautiful young woman on a wide couch being taken from behind by a muscular young fellow. Receiving and giving at the same time she masturbated a sitting man, while sucking the cock of a third standing alongside. Several other people stood close by, watching, touching, stroking her tits and fondling the mens' balls.

I passed an elderly man sitting alone on a small chair, his hand thrashing up and down his erection, completely lost in his own little selfish world.

Although dressed – or undressed – for the party in see-through dress and thong, I avoided all entanglements and offers. Although I admit it hard to stay out of a mass orgy going on in a special dark room, once my eyes adjusted to the gloom. A seething pile of bodies rolled and struggled in a truly magnificent multi-sex ballet in combinations of remarkable ingenuity.

But that must wait until another time when I'm not working and can relax and join in.

Feeling I could be wasting my time here – everyone far too busy to talk – I stopped at a bar. Sitting on a bench sipping my drink, watching the crowd rolling by seeking or participating in continual sex I prepared to give up and leave. This seemed the wrong place to find anyone with information on The Bishop.

Then luck fell on me again. A small well-muscled man with thick black eyebrows and tiny intelligent eyes flopped down beside me. Without a word he lifted my skirt, pushed my thong aside, and slithered finger and thumb up and down one of my labia. It felt quite pleasant so I opened slightly to make it easier and reaching for his erection, started to play with long slow strokes.

After a couple of seconds he leaned close and whispered, 'I'm not really interested in this shit. Are you?'

'Do you mean the sex or the whole place?'

'Both. It's all so fuckin' manufactured.'

'Then why are you here?'

'I'm a journalist. I'm investigating the criminals running this stupid shebang. It's taking ages and I'm sick to death of the whole job. I think I'll give up and go home.'

'Are you married?

'No.'

'Then I'll come with you. We can talk and fuck properly there. And help each other with the criminals.

'Ok.'

I slipped my thong back into place, pulled down my skirt and followed.

Chapter 12

We found our overcoats and hailed a taxi.

'Where do you live?' he asked.

'In a hotel. It's better we go to your place.'

Leaning close he whispered, 'How can you help me with the criminals?'

'Later. Once we're away from prying ears.'

He nodded, held my hand and dozed for the short journey to a suburb, making no move to touch me up.

Leading me into his apartment on the fifth floor – 'Safer up here, away from the goons,' – he fetched two beers and settled beside me.

'Shoot,' he said.

'No, you go first. You're the journalist. I'm only a travel writer.'

His black-beetle eyebrows shot up. 'A travel writer? What the fuck's a travel writer doing chasing criminals?

So I decided to go first; told him about an assignment to write a pornographic travel book taking in sex clubs and major brothels across Europe; told him that in Nice I came across a criminal called... here I pretended to forget his name... 'The priest, or the monk or something...'

'Oh God. You're trying to find out about The bastard Bishop?'

'The Bishop. Yes. That's the man. Yes, I want to interview him for my book. Where do I find him?'

'Find him? *Find him?* If you try to find him, he'll find you first.'

'So you know him?'

'Not personally. Apart from his wife and girl friends, no-one knows him personally.'

'But you know *of* him?'

He snuggled close, put an arm round me and began to fondle my breast.

'Listen darling. You are best to stay away from this guy. Let me tell you why...'

Still fondling, he told me of a team of investigating journalists; 'Me and three others set up to investigate The Bishop. No one would talk except one man. He knew something and dropped a few hints but after a few weeks my three mates were dead, with me the only survivor.'

'How did you survive?'

'Because my job to stay safe in the office and write up their notes kept me out of sight while the others nosed around.'

'How did they die?'

'That doesn't matter. They died and I didn't. So I let the whole thing drop. No-one will ever be able to pin it on The Bishop. He simply arranges one way or another to rub out anyone asking questions. Don't even *try* getting close or you'll go too.'

Wiggling my breast against his massaging hand, I said, 'Perhaps they died because they were men. Perhaps it's easier for a woman to get close.'

'Perhaps. But don't do it.'

'Why is he called The Bishop?

'He's always a move or two ahead in every game he plays. He works everything out and shifts his men around so not even they know understand the whole game or their part in it. That's why they're called Chessmen.'

'Oh,' I said. 'That's clever. I saw a part picture of him in a newspaper – just an arm and an ear. Nothing you could recognise beyond a big gold watch and some hair strands across his ear. The hair looked black, so he must be quite young.'

'Or he may use dye.'

The hand on my breast became more insistent. The other hand stroked down under my thong and began to pull and play with my bush.

'Look, darling,' he said, with an extra tug, 'Let's change the subject and make sure we survive. Why don't we go and try a few games of our own.'

So I let him take me to bed where he howled with joy during a Class Two Thai I gave before sliding on. We both came several times during the massage and the following fuck. I must say I enjoyed it as much as he did.

In the middle of all I brought him to the edge of ecstasy twice and stopped.

'Why?' he groaned with a shudder.

'So you'll promise to introduce me to the man with more information.'

The first time he said, 'Never.'

The second time – tortured beyond imagining – he surrendered and in slavish gratitude offered a bonus.

'I'll give you my investigation notes,' he sighed.

Finally exhausted I let him sleep. We coiled together, made supple as a couple of snakes by those hours of sex.

Chapter 13

Next morning he left for work and I went shopping.

My plan to save time by drawing The Bishop's Chessmen onto me needed careful organisation.

In street markets I bought cheap second-hand clothes. From a theatrical dealer I bought a black spiky wig to copy Dominique's hair and stage makeup for easy transfer from ruddy faced country-girl Simone to suntanned elegant Eleanor or poor pale Dominique, so ill and wan.

I trundled my purchases back to my hotel, entering as Simone and leaving as Eleanor, carrying a neat expensive travel bag. By taxi Eleanor went to one of the most expensive hotels in Paris and took a suite overlooking the Seine, paying cash for a three week stay. She left as pale, unremarkable Dominique, ignored by snooty staff; unseen by Paris hurrying by.

Dominique took a bus to a poor downtrodden suburb full of poor downtrodden people and paid rent for a three week stay in a flea-bitten hotel with exits on two parallel streets.

She then went by bus to the nearest main station and in the toilets changed back to Simone, finding it really difficult to clean off the damned greasepaint caught behind the ears and along the hairline.

By late afternoon Simone sat drinking coffee outside a smart cafe opposite Journalist's flat. I saw his fingers ripple the window blinds and guessed he peeped out to make sure I had turned up.

A minute later he came to the door but instead of stepping out and hurrying over he stayed half-hidden, checking up and down the street, peering at every car parked within a hundred metres before scuttling across.

Without stopping he hurried past into the cafe, hissing, 'Inside. Quick. We can't sit out here.'

'What's wrong?' I asked, joining him in a corner where he sat hunched; his black eyebrows curved into a frightened frown.

'I couldn't get the notes. They've disappeared.'

'Why are you so worried?'

'Those notes killed my friends. Where are they now? It worries me to death that they're out in the open again. I managed to sneak into the editorial office and look for them without anyone seeing me. At least I think so. But those notes were tucked away in a secret and secure place. But someone's stolen them and may have passed them on. Perhaps The Bishop has them now. He'll be looking for me.'

'Are you saying someone in your office informed to The Bishop?'

'Who else would have? The operation stayed secret even after the murders. Only the crime editor knew what we were doing – he'd thought up the idea – and I've just heard he's dead too. Driving home yesterday; went over a big cliff into the sea. Real freak of an accident, hey?'

The cafe door opened. He flinched, dipping his head in an effort to hide. He'd never manage with those eyebrows, poor soul.

After a few sips of thick black coffee he improved and offered a little grin. 'You probably think I'm exaggerating and I may be, but that new death really freaked me. I may be ok. No-one but the crime editor knew I had anything to do with the investigation.'

'Can anyone connect you to the notes?'

'I doubt it. They were computer generated and could have been written by anyone. Do you think that makes it ok?'

'Do you mean no-one at all knew your part in the investigation, or only no-one in the newsroom?'

'Well, my police friend knew. He's an Inspector in the crime department. I thought he might be able to get at some information for us.'

'When do I meet this man?'

'I've arranged it for this evening. He'll come to your hotel at eight.'

'*My hotel?* How does he know my hotel? *You* don't know my hotel.'

'This morning he had you followed when you left my apartment.'

'But he doesn't know what I look like.'

'Oh yes he does. We were together in the sex club five metres along the bar from you. He tossed a coin to see which of us would touch you up and I won.'

'You *tossed a coin for me?*'

'Yup.' He shrugged, obviously embarrassed.

I could have killed him there and then but too many people would notice, so I slapped him playfully.

'And the policeman had me followed?'

'Seems like it.'

'Alright. I'll meet him at eight. What does he look like?'

'Doesn't matter. Stay in the bar and he'll come to you. Let me know how you get on. I'll try find out a few more things today.'

I nodded. He left, scampering back to the safety of his apartment.

So. The Police Inspector will come to me.
This one sounds intelligent and dangerous.
I'll need to be careful.

Chapter 14

Just before eight, sitting by a window in the bar, I watched a smartly dressed man – very confident and sure – stride from a chauffeur driven car to salutes from the two doormen.

This must be my Police Inspector.

His car drew away. He chatted easily at the concierge desk, checked his watch and nodded when they pointed me out through the glass partition.

'I think we have an appointment,' he said. 'Let me buy you a drink.'

'I don't want to talk here.'

'Shall we go to your room?'

'No. A bar.'

I'd already chosen a place nearby. Small, dark, noisy; oozing with dubious charm and ringed by tiny almost private booths – perfect for smooching lovers, whispered conversation and exchanging secrets and plans.

He chose a booth and pulled back a chair. I pushed past and took a padded bench with my back to the wall.

'I enjoy people-watching.'

He shrugged, settled down facing me and examined my face. I returned the compliment, studying his olive-brown skin, almost black eyes and sharp cheekbones. With black oiled-down hair and well honed shoulders his origins seemed Italian, possibly Spanish, perhaps Corsican.

He certainly showed the tight self-confident arrogance of Mediterranean man.

Add a silly little moustache and he could be a smaller edition of my Chessman in Nice.

'Who are you?' he demanded.

'I'm here for conversation not interrogation. Who are you?'

He broke into a smile of unexpected charm.

'You already know. I am an Inspector of Police. I believe you also know that with a little more luck we may have met last night.'

'Your luck or mine?'

'Mine, naturally.'

'Alright, I'll tell you. I'm a travel writer commissioned to write about the European sex scene. I need detail on how brothels and sex clubs are run. I understand most of them have criminal connections – Mafia or gangs from the East. I asked our friend the Journalist about a man I heard of in Nice with some religious connection.'

'Ah yes. The Bishop. No religion involved I'm afraid. He is very, very, *very* criminal and very, very, *very* dangerous. It is best you stay away and ask no questions.'

I shook my head.

He sighed and with a delicate shrug whispered, 'I really and truly advise you. Don't become involved with this man in any way. Relax and enjoy your time in Paris. Perhaps spend some time with me?'

'I'd spend time with you if you answer some questions for my book.'

Again the charming smile. Quite handsome really.

He nodded. 'Go ahead. Ask.'

I launched into a series of pretty easy requests for information about the sex trade in general. He suggested he take me to another sex club to help my research in the right surroundings, 'But ask no questions about criminals who may run these places. And especially ask none about The Bishop.'

'Why not?'

'Evil surrounds him. And he removes people who cross him, hunt for him or ask about him.'

'Where does he come from?'

'No-one knows.'

'Where does he live?'

'No-one is sure. He shifts between many houses and apartments.

'Does he have business here in Paris?'

'People asking questions have certainly died in Paris. And his own people who change sides meet fast and awful death.'

'Including a young couple shot, mutilated and washed ashore near Nice recently?'

Obviously startled he leaned forward and snapped, 'They agreed to testify against him. Traitors deserve what they get.'

I couldn't stop a brief flash of satisfaction crossing my face. He sat back, stiff and silent for a moment, then said, 'I must keep quiet about this man. Police enquiries are ongoing.'

We parted a few minutes later, agreeing to meet again.

He gave me his card. 'Call me when you're free.'

I watched his firm buttocks roll away through the evening crowd.

Rather dishy. A pity I don't trust him.

And because I don't trust him I followed.

He stopped by a news stand and spoke to a short nondescript man who nodded and walked away. He pulled out a mobile phone and made an agitated call, hands waving, face screwed and angry. Why?

I think he's reporting in. I think he thinks he's onto me.

Time to tool up.

Chapter 15

I sent a coded message through my Cloud Mail-Box and went back to my hotel. On the way in I noticed a short nondescript man at the bus stop. Half an hour later when I emerged as the elegant Eleanor and stepped into a taxi, he didn't look; didn't move.

Returning to Eleanor's expensive hotel suite I sat at the desk and fell into deep thought.

Although I don't trust Police Inspector I now have four men and three women to juggle in working out a plan to close in on The Bishop. A plan needs close detail using, for the time being, two bankers, one journalist and one copper.

The bankers are expendable, the journalist important; the copper suspect.

Only Eleanor and Simone can be out in the open – Dominique must remain a shadow.

I made a few notes and diagrams, matching the three women to the four men. Banker One knows me as Simone, simple country girl, Banker Two knows me as the rich and elegant Eleanor. Journalist and Police Inspector know me as Simone the travel writer.

To keep out of the way and let things stew in my head, I spent three days as Eleanor, visiting The Louvre, the Opera and several expensive shops, buying jewellery and more clothes, acting the wealthy woman in Paris on holiday. Several obviously rich men tried to pick up this exquisite creature alone in the big city but she always dodged their advances with grace and charm, accepting their cards with a promise to call.

Then I went back to work. As Eleanor I called Banker Two. His secretary burst into tears when I asked to speak.

'He's dead,' she said. 'He drowned in the Seine yesterday.'

I cut the call without giving my name.

'*They've killed him*,' I told my image in the mirror. *'He wasn't as clever as he thought.'*

I switched on the television.

"Young Banker with great future dragged dead from the river. Enormous loss to the world of finance. Must have been mugged as heavy wounds to the head. Forensics and autopsy will show whether killed by beating or drowning..."

'It'll be the beating to make sure,' I told my image. *'It's possible he could swim.'*

I stopped conversing with myself and the implications. Main point is that his death shows no trail to me. Should I be sorry for the arrogant devil? No. He probably showed off in a bar and the stinking low-life criminal who didn't scare him sent his thugs. So much for being far too clever to be caught by such a man.

Switching to Simone I called Banker One and found him alive and oh, so happy to hear from me and when can we have dinner again?

'Soon,' I said. 'Have you anything for me?'

'No. Sorry. I worried at breaking the Bank's rules. I couldn't bring myself to do it. But please can we have dinner again?'

'Of course. I'll meet you tomorrow evening. Same place as before, at eight.'

Such delight in his voice for such disappointment to follow. But at least his old mother won't lose her son.

Journalist next. No answer from his apartment so I called the newsroom. 'We haven't seen him for a couple of days,' said an anxious sounding young woman. 'It's unusual that he doesn't ring in but we're not worried yet. He met a new girlfriend a few days ago and think he may be away somewhere with her.'

Well now. They know something's happening and they know a woman is involved. For several seconds I worried then cast him from my mind. He's big enough to care for himself.

I called Police Inspector. He said, 'Sure, let's meet the day after tomorrow. I'll collect you at ten for dinner and some late night education.'

So only one of my four workers survives and I can guess why.

I moved back to Simone's hotel and checked my Cloud Mail-Box.

Packet in Monaco said the message and gave me the address and details of a special, very secret safe deposit box.

Good. I've always wanted to see Monte Carlo.

Chapter 16

Eleanor went by train to Monte Carlo and checked in her small travel case then took a taxi from the station to a large shopping area and wandered in. Such a woman is not out of place surrounded by all this expensive luxury.

Of course, being beautifully dressed right down to a pair of soft white gloves, I fitted in perfectly.

I strolled through the indoor boulevards without a care in the world, window shopping and popping in to buy a few items that caught my eye. Each purchase gave me time to check for followers or watchers.

Once certain I had no tail, I wandered into a shop selling quite pornographic lingerie at prices aimed at the super-rich. Only women absolutely loaded with money would enter, so the place is as secure as a high-class bank.

To protect browsing millionaires' wives from view, swathes of expensive soft-silk drapes rippled from the ceiling and a total absence of cameras made the shopping experience ultra-private.

I looked at a few naughty bras and knickers near the door and checked for possible followers watching through the window, then drifted deeper into the shop and the maze of moving drapes. A beautiful assistant ushered me from display to display, pointing, suggesting and discussing colours.

Loaded with half a dozen delicate items she led me into a velvet walled changing room. Before leaving she touched a hidden button. A tall mirror swung back revealing a small porch and elevator.

I went down through what must have been several hundred metres to a stunning bejewelled cave carved into rock. 'Welcome to reception,' said a young man dressed in the most exquisite suit you can imagine.

'How do you know I'm me?' I asked. 'Where is your security?'

Smiling he said, 'You've passed through security in several ways since you left your taxi. Your friends sent us full electronic details and our systems are never wrong.'

He stopped at a wall covered in ranks of large metal boxes.

Handing me a sliver of rice paper with two lines of numbers, he said, 'When you enter your box release code the secure examination-room door behind us opens automatically. The room is soundproof, bomb-proof and has no cameras or any other way of identifying you for us or for anyone else. Please make sure you keep your gloves on for finger-print and DNA protection. Touch nothing without them.'

He bowed and left.

I entered fifty-two numbers and symbols. My box slid from the wall. At the same time I heard a sigh of movement as the door behind me opened.

In the examination room I used a thirty number code to open the box. No wonder it weighed so little. The clever devils had sent me exactly what I wanted, all in miniature.

I lifted out two tiny hand-guns and a knife disguised as a lipstick with blade hidden in the handle and several small transparent packets.

All three weapons I remembered from training, described by the Instructor as, 'Perfect assassination weapons for perfect killing. Up close, unexpected and immediate. That's the way to do it.'

Finally I lifted out four packets of different coloured powders, each a terrible poison from the forests of South America.

I sighed with delight.

Now I am *really* able to go to work.

Chapter 17

Collecting my travel case from the station I went to the most expensive hotel my taxi driver knew and booked a suite for three nights.

Sitting in the enclosed veranda overlooking the yacht harbour, I sipped wine and savoured the view, deliberately ignoring my expensively packed box of lacy underwear, also containing my new toys. Leave that pleasure till later.

But after five minutes I could no longer wait. I unpacked and tried on my new lust-inducing lingerie; dinky little thongs, nipple-revealing bras, knickers and suspender belts, the sheerest of sheer stockings.

I especially liked the thong stippled with tiny jewels, twinkling as I twitched my hips.

Oh, how *sexy* I looked. Enough to drive any man wild when I do a catwalk parade for his pleasure.

And my own pleasure as it turned out.

Admiring my perfect reflection in the mirror I began to ache for a spare sexy yacht millionaire so we could test things out. But I took hold of myself – mentally, not physically – and insisted to my reflection that I get back to work.

So I unpacked my weapons and spread them out.

Two miniature automatic pistols of unique design made from high tensile plastic toughened to gun-metal strength impossible to detect on any security device. Without triggers or hammers both operated in almost complete silence.

The first used special projectile made from the same gun-metal plastic. Held in a six-shot magazine that clicked into the handle, the projectiles have no cartridge or explosive charge to go bang and send them on their way.

Instead, designed as a mini-rocket, a small switch on the grip sparks to ignite liquid fuel. With a slight sneeze the rocket shoots at twice the muzzle speed of a normal bullet for a range of about four metres.

A needle-sharp nose penetrates thick skull bone or Kevlar body armour with ease. Once in head or body a small explosive charge pops and pulps every internal organ nearby, shattering the slug to dust and leaving a forensic nightmare with no evidence or hint of the weapon used.

The second pistol is exactly the same design but uses highly charged compressed air to shoot a tiny poison-covered dart at the same speed. The dart is useless against bone or body armour and works only against soft flesh. The dart also explodes on contact, leaving no trace of dart or quick-acting, quick-dispersing poison.

Target dies within three seconds and by the time forensics get to work nothing remains to show cause of death; another nightmare for the poor scientists. By causing apparent natural death, dart gun is probably the best stealth weapon.

The lipstick-knife is another almost perfect assassination tool. A small button whips the blade out for immediate penetration into throat, artery or spinal column without effort. Not so good if others know you are with Target at dinner or a function and can be recognised later, but great for anonymous murder in a crowd.

Finally the poisons.

Oh how efficient they are and how terrible in their application. Sprinkled on food or drink or smeared as paste on the tip of a blade, these silent killers work within seconds and without pain. No gurgles or groans to alert nearby security.

Now, feeling properly tooled I decided to spend the rest of my Monte Carlo holiday in restaurants and casinos, seeking out a millionaire or two to share the delights of my new lingerie outfits.

Then back north to my first Paris victim – a short nondescript man who stands by a bus stop and has probably seen and remembered too much.

Chapter 18

After three nights of gambling and debauchery – two millionaires and one big yacht – I relaxed and recovered on the train to Paris in the character of Simone.

Walking into my hotel I glanced across at the bus stop. No sign of Short Nondescript Man. I rested, showered and planned in my room for a couple of hours then went out to buy a newspaper and saw Short Nondescript Man standing in his usual position.

So we have an informer in the hotel. The message *'Madame Dubois has returned,'* must have been passed instantly.

Time to act.

At eight that evening Dominique stood waiting for a bus; one insignificant patch of evening shadow among other insignificant bus queue shadows.

I managed to shuffle alongside Short Nondescript Man.

A bus came.

I raised my arm to show I wanted to get on and pushing past shot a poisoned dart into his neck before hopping through the door and squeezing in with a crowd of impatient Parisians hurrying home.

No seat, so I stood and looked back as Short Nondescript Man began to topple. In true Parisian style those around him skipped out of the way and let him fall.

This is the first time I saw the poisons work in real life, so to speak. They really are very good and I must recommend them along with those neat little darts.

I left the bus after three stops and walked back. At the hotel I watched an ambulance pull away and wondered if Police Inspector would replace his street spy.

And I wondered if Police Inspector would connect the timing of my return to Short Nondescript Man's departure.

I changed back to Simone and called his number.

'Where have you been?' he asked.

'None of your business. I just travelled for a few days. I *am* a travel writer you know.'

He chuckled. 'If you're going to be so aggressive I won't invite you to dinner and another sex club. How about tonight?'

'No. I'm tired from travelling. Tomorrow will do.'

'Ok. I'll collect you at eight.'

Next morning at breakfast I read about the disappearance of a well-known journalist. Flattening out newspaper I followed the story over three pages. It started with a broad assumption of kidnapping.

Journalist Abducted

One of our famous investigative reporting team is missing. He has not been seen for over a week. **The** Sole Survivor *of our four man team investigating a major criminal and his associates, he has now himself disappeared without trace, feared abducted and murdered by the same killers who ended the lives of his three colleagues over a period of five days last month. Detectives found only one of the other three murdered journalists, probably displayed as a warning...*

The article went on to describe his childhood, education, previous journalistic successes and examples of his previous investigations, mainly financial and political. It gave his real name and details of his wife and three children, with plenty of photographs to pad the story out.

So it turns out the newspaper threw my Journalist from the financial section into crime at the deep end. Being inexperienced may have cost him his life and it seems unlikely he'll resurface in good condition, or resurface at all, poor fellow.

But my life must go on so I telephoned Police Inspector, 'Just to confirm eight this evening.'

'Fine,' he said. 'Don't wear too many clothes. You're not allowed in those clubs properly dressed.'

'Don't worry. I'll make sure I'm barely covered and completely available.'

'Just what I hoped for.'

Chapter 19

Dressed for the occasion – dinner first then sex club – I waited in the bar for Police Inspector.

'That's a beautiful cloak you're wearing. What's underneath?'

'Not much. I'm just about naked.'

I stood, flipped the elegant hood over my hair and twirled to show off the expensive burgundy-red material swirling around my legs with a heavy satisfying feel.

'No one would ever know I'm dressed and ready for hot action after dinner.'

'Or during,'

'Who knows?'

We both giggled. Lovers making arrangements.

He chose a dark-panelled poorly lit restaurant that seemed a replica of the bar from a few days ago – private booths and smoochy couples – what could be better for a slow dinner and a quick fumble?

I sat on the wall-bench facing out. He sat opposite, leaning forward and concentrating on my face with those strange almost-black eyes, his sharp cheeks and honey coloured skin somehow emphasised by the low light.

'Are you married?' he asked.

'No personal questions tonight,' I said. 'This is an arm's length evening. More later if we get to know each other. Are we being followed or watched now?'

'Why do you ask?

'You had me followed the other night so I don't trust you.'

He rolled back and laughed, his lovely strong shoulders hunched.

'I only did that to make sure we could do this.'

'No more following or watching then?

'I promise.'

After a delectable dinner eaten, wonderful wine sipped and appreciated, midnight came, 'Soon time to go clubbing but first a few official questions,' he said.

'What do you need to know?'

'For your own protection I must ask – why are you so interested in The Bishop?'

'I've already told you. I'm a writer. '

'But it seems wrong that a beautiful woman places herself in danger by foolishly hunting a vicious criminal. Unless you have another reason for this chase.

'What other reason would I have? I want to get close to see him, to speak to him, perhaps become one of his personal whores. I understand he has several as well as a wife. That would be a great line of chapters for my book.'

'Would you truly do that?'

'Why not? I've already worked several months in high class brothels and for a couple of call-girl outfits to see how they operate. And now I'm going to sex clubs for the same reason. Sleeping with the Bishop is just an extension of my research.'

'My God, you're definitely on your way to the morgue. Anyway, you'll need to be on the Riviera. He's hardly ever in Paris.'

'Where on the Riviera, it's a long coast?'

'Nice. Have you been to Nice?'

'Passed through.'

His eyes narrowed. His face switched from prospective lover to enquiring policeman.

'When were you there? I know that a woman spent some time in Nice, following one of The Bishop's men. But she wasn't like you. I am told she looked like a poor woman from the *bidonvilles*. Perhaps with a grudge, because an Arab friend of The Bishop's died checking up on her. She must have lured him into a trap for a relative or gang friend to blow away. Did you discover anything about this during your travel book research?'

'No. I only heard about the supposed young lovers you called traitors the other day.'

'Ah yes. The Bishop always makes sure witnesses against him don't get to court, one way or another.'

'Did he ever catch the *bidonvilles* woman?'

'No. She disappeared. For all we know she's dead. By the way, did you see a commotion outside your hotel yesterday evening? Can you tell me any detail?'

'Not really. I saw an ambulance but don't know what happened. Anyway. Why are we talking of these things? We're supposed to be enjoying ourselves. Stop being a policeman and start being a lover.'

'We're talking because I hope you saw or heard something. One of my plainclothes men died at the bus stop opposite your hotel. If you were there you may have witnessed the incident.'

'Why on earth should I be at a bus stop? For God's sake come and sit next to me for a coffee before we go.'

He came round and sat on the bench. We sipped with one hand and stroked under the table with the other. His apparently expensive suit, designed for sex clubs, came apart at various places, making surreptitious fondling easy.

I shivered with pleasure at his expert fingering and allowed it to go on. I wanted to get most possible enjoyment out of the evening because what he just told me makes our affair doomed before it starts.

Now I feel he is putting two and two together.
Now I feel he is definitely on to me.
Now I feel he is working for The Bishop.
Now I feel it's time to see him off.

Chapter 20

He escorted me to a new sex club in an area of narrow streets near my hotel. We left our outer clothes at reception and entered the same louche and disgusting world as before. They could have been the same people acting out the same fantasies and sex games in the same rooms and at the same intensity.

After twenty minutes of being stroked and massaged and explored by half a dozen different men and women I felt cold and frigid towards the whole scene. My Police Inspector disappeared into an orgy room and returned with two semi-naked young women attached to his arms.

'How about a foursome?'
'No. I've seen enough. I'm going.'
'It'll be fun.'
'No. I'm tired of this. I'm off.'
'I'll come too. I don't want to lose sight of you.'
'Lose sight of me? What does that mean?'
'Nothing. A slip of the tongue. What I mean is I want our evening to continue.'
'If you wish. But I want to walk. I need the fresh air.'
'Ok.'

At two hours past midnight, we strolled along dark and empty streets.

Clutching his arm in almost loving embrace I nuzzled at his neck and whispered soft kisses on his cheek. The corner of my eye caught two young men in dark clothes following on silent shoes.

Paris Chessmen perhaps?

Now how does a young girl wearing only a thong under a cloak protect herself from a planned kill?

Using soft masking tape she attaches a miniature dart gun in the cave of her left armpit. This means she can dance, eat, drink, wave to friends and hug her lover provided she only raises her right arm. The practiced assassin can release and shoot in a split second.

She also finds a way to check where her murderous lover hides his gun. A few hugs and cuddles answers the question.

So when *my* murderous lover, apparently overcome with passion, pulled me into a dark alley, pressed me against the wall and pulled open my heavy cloak in sexual frenzy. I allowed him to get started.

As soon as the soft patter of almost silent shoes speeded from walk to trot I released my dart gun, whispered, 'You're right. I killed your fat Arab friend in Nice,' and popped a little arrow into that soft hollow below his Adam's apple.

In the seconds before he fell his eyes widened and his mouth opened but he died before he could speak.

I let him slump, followed him down and, crouching, waited for my two counter-assassins. They hurried into the alley, slowed to check their target and seeing only a shadowy pile on the floor walked forward.

They bent close to see what had happened.

I hit them with a dart each. In silence they fell.

Using the edge of my cloak to cover fingerprints, I took one of their guns and shot a bullet into Police Inspector's forehead. Although well dead, his blood still flowed into a quite satisfactory dark pool on the pebbles.

Lifting out Police Inspector's pistol I shot my two amateur assassins, one in the face, one in the chest. Again plenty of blood.

Quite pleased with myself I curled Police Inspector's fingers round his pistol grip and left my two assassin's guns where they dropped.

I stood back and looked at my handiwork, pleased with the puzzle I'd left both forensics and detectives.

Work that one out boys.

Leaving no sign that anyone other than those three men had been in the alley, I walked through to the other end and followed empty streets to my hotel.

Next morning I packed, paid and left.

At Eleanor's hotel I did the same.

There I abandoned Simone and faded back into Dominique.

Covering my small suitcase with an old blanket I went by bus to Dominique's flea-bitten hotel and stayed for two days, burning Eleanor's and Simone's fashionable clothes on rubbish dumps around the area. Otherwise I stayed off the streets, except for going out to a nearby cafe to eat.

On the third day I wrapped Dominique's few shabby possessions bundled into a stained grey blanket tied with string and went by bus to The Riviera.

Chapter 21

Three days of relaxing travel from Paris to Cote d'Azure gave me opportunity to think and plan how to get alongside The Bishop. I wondered if the realisation that he is being hunted by a woman has yet dawned.

My Chessman in Nice will certainly have mentioned the drab little woman who turned up a couple of times and last seen leading the now dead Arab into the shadows.

If Police Inspector reported a woman asking questions in Paris, The Bishop may consider it strange and tie the Arab's departure to Police Inspector's departure.

On the other hand newspaper reports of my Police Inspector's death made it clear that detectives had an open-and-shut gang killing. Sensational headlines followed by equally breathless copy shouted the exciting news.

Famous Detective Dies In Gang Shootout

Brave crime fighter shot dead doing what he loved best – fighting filthy criminals from the Paris cess pits. Famous detective dies trying to arrest two lizards from the underworld slime, killing two from a gang of half a dozen attacking him in a dark alley...

This great *story* spun on and on giving details of his life as an incorruptible police officer of a type all too rare these days. *Knowing he had a cruel and desperate gang cornered he called for armed assistance but couldn't wait before taking them on alone in his duty to save **The People Of Paris** from these scum.*

The Paris police certainly want to squeeze as much credit as possible from the killing of an officer they must have known as corrupt. They're probably all the same and this wonderful twisted story keeps their Force a dedicated and respected body of men – brave and honest to a fault – willing to die for their duty to **The People Of Paris**.

Thanks guys.

You've probably saved me fatal embarrassment by keeping me under wraps and failing to mention that this wonderful upstanding officer spent time during his last few hours in this world pleasuring me in a restaurant

Nor did you mention that this extremely upstanding officer spent his final hour using his extremely upstanding tool pleasuring multiple women in a sex club.

I searched and searched through the paper to find any mention of a Small Nondescript Man leaving us via an unexplained death at a bus stop.

Not a word.

So thanks again guys. Two policemen dying in the streets near or with a woman may have been too much of a coincidence for The Bishop to miss.

I took one day off in Lyon to rest and think, strolling round the beautiful city and along the river bank. No one tried to pick up dull little Dominique – not one man even bothered to look at the colourless waif wandering by.

At Lyon, decisions made.

No more Simone. She's done enough in Paris. Sorry, girl, it's goodbye forever.

Dominique? You must hang around for a while in case needed. But be a good girl and stay in the shadows. We'll buy a simple apartment for you in the poorest suburb. Go there and stay until called.

Eleanor? Your big part in this whole performance is about to start.

You must be ready to take centre stage.
You must be ready to shine in the spotlight.
You must be ready to love and to kill.
The killing is easy. Love can only be acted.
But you can do it, girl.

Chapter 22

I used the final leg of my bus journey plotting Eleanor's entry to the society of Cote d'Azure millionaires or – even better – billionaires.

I think I need a more likely method of getting alongside The Bishop than simply killing my way up the ladder to complete my contract. I need a new approach.

While passing through the lush Provencal countryside Eleanor developed in my head as a rich, fashionable American heiress with all the trimmings – large villa, cooks and servants, plenty of money when Daddy dies but – poor girl – she's lonely.

Oh how she wanted company.

Oh, how she wanted a good time with good friends.

Oh, how she wanted true love.

Oh, how she wanted a husband; preferably with more money than Daddy plans to land on her by dying.

Eleanor will certainly be more fun than either the late Simone or shy little Dominique. I think I'll enjoy being Eleanor.

At a large, fashionable town a few kilometres short of Nice I stepped from the bus and ditched Dominique's dirty bundle in a back-street skip and bought a cheap dress in the market.

Then at a shop a notch or two up from the market stall, bought a better quality dress and in a richer part of town moved up another couple of notches in both shop and quality. This progressive upward motion continued for several hours while dowdy Dominique changed magically to elegant Eleanor without anyone noticing.

When the merry-go-round ended I called a taxi and drove to the best hotel in Nice, booked in and began my campaign.

Chapter 23

First I made it known around estate agents that I needed a luxury villa.

Offers flooded in. I decided on a lovely place in the hills behind the town. With money shifted from Paris, the place bought and servants chosen, I started my luxurious life of a rich but lonely American heiress.

Buying the villa emptied and closed the account held by Bank One. With Banker Two dead, no one in Paris will remember me, except Journalist, if he's still alive.

My new Bishop search began by going to Casinos and making myself obvious by betting high, drinking hard, and flirting with anyone who looked rich and criminal enough to move in The Bishop's circle.

But most well-heeled men I met were either drunken horny businessmen looking for a quick lay or ultra-rich Arabs wanting women for nights of sex that included all kinds of strange Middle-Eastern practices.

To keep in practice I slept with several of both types; making sure I stayed in character as a scatty American unsure of Europe; not too experienced in the way of this exciting new world outside good old USA, but available and open for any kind of sex.

I had plenty of lecherous offers from the obvious crooks and gangsters who swarmed the casinos. Once, in the half light of Monaco Casino, I thought I saw Chessman and turned away. I couldn't be sure because so many of his type look alike.

After a couple of weeks I felt bored with losing a sledge load of cash every night with no result other than lying on my back, my front, bending over or kneeling; being tickled, slapped; acting the masochist or sadist for a series of poor deluded souls and wondered if my new plan is a dud.

Would I be better to bring Dominique out and murder a few of The Bishop's thugs and start them looking for me? Before they died I'd probably be able to frighten something out of them to get me nearer my Target.

Then luck took over. While concentrating on the cards a soft hand slid over my shoulder.

Quite pleasant. A hand to be massaged by.

A voice whispered, 'My friend wants to meet you.'

'Bugger off,' I said to the short homosexual with startling pink hair and expensive jewellery. 'I don't do queer.'

'Tut-tut, Sweetie,' he murmured with a giggle and a pout. 'How *terribly* normal.'

He puffed me a kiss. 'I'll be back. My friend is persistent and horribly, *horribly* straight. You'll like him.'

Back he came the next night, this time with blue hair and luxurious make up.

'Oh *do* come for an introduction and sip of expensive wine.' he said. 'You'll love the dear old thing. He's great fun and very rich.'

'Bugger off.'

Back he came the next night, hair again pink and a jacket of shining zigzag stripes.

'Like it? A present from my friend. Oh he is *so* generous. Do come and meet him.'

At that moment a tight-bunched group of heavies marched through the casino, surrounding and almost hiding a short hurrying man. I saw only a few strands of hair but realised – my Target – here is my Target. In the same building and in view...

Who's that?' I asked Little Queer.

'Oh, he's a terrible man. Mind you I mustn't be too rude. He's a friend of my friend.

'Where is your friend?'

A manicured finger pointed.

'But he's old.'

'Ah yes. But still active. You'll love him Sweetie. He's such a darling man. And rich.'

'I don't care about rich. I'm a millionaire.'

'Oh Sweetie, is that all? *Only* a millionaire? Poor you. My friend trumps that by several billion. Well lots of billions actually.'

'Take me to him.'

Chapter 24

I saw immediately that my handsome, white haired, smoothy of an Old Billionaire had oodles of charm and oodles of cash. I couldn't guess his age but both body and wallet seemed in excellent shape.

Within minutes we were old friends. I stroked his hand, he stroked my hair. We whispered secrets and lies – mostly lies – and sort of fell in love.

'I meet many, many women,' he murmured, 'But you are the most beautiful.'

'Do you sleep with them all?'

'Of course. Will you come home with me tonight?'

'Naturally.'

'Oh, he'll love you,' giggled Little Queer. 'He hates the ones who play hard to get.'

'For three nights I've watched you,' said Old Billionaire. 'You're very rash. You lose a lot. I shall teach you to gamble.'

'Please do. Can you introduce me into society too? I am lonely here and need friends.'

'Of course. It will be my pleasure. By the way, I love your American accent. So cultured; so educated.'

And so false, old boy. But it certainly works.

'Oh, darling,' lisped Little Queer. 'You've made such a hit. Even I'm attracted. You almost make me wish I'd been born straight.'

We went to the Baccarat table and Old Billionaire showed me how to play cards above the table with his right hand whilst playing using his left to play with me below the table. At one point I had to whisper, 'Stop, darling. You'll make me come.'

It is true. He played both cards and me so expertly, that I only managed to avoid a thunderous orgasm by breaking into a fit of coughing. His delicate fingering stopped and I managed to bring myself down with a shiver of regret.

'My God, you Frenchmen,' I whispered.'

'A lot more of that when we get home,' he murmured with a wink.

And I must say, he knew how to excite a girl. Before we went to bed he sniffed some fancy concoction – 'It'll make me strong as a lion' – he chuckled.

It certainly did. He kept me at it until well after dawn although by the time Little Queer entered with breakfast Old Billionaire looked about ninety.

I took my croissants, orange juice and coffee out onto an enormous sunlit terrace jutting over a steep cliff. Elbows on balcony I looked down through beautiful turquoise surface water shining clear as an early morning mirror. A few metres down, the colour changed to cold, quite frightening, dark blue.

Little Queer joined me, pulling together a gorgeous silk dressing gown.

'Beautiful isn't it?' he said.

'The sea or your gown?'

'Both', he giggled.

I said, 'Look at how the colours merge. The deeper it goes the darker the colour until it is almost black.'

'The cliff goes fifty metres from here to the sea then straight on down for over two hundred metres to rocks at the bottom.'

I sat back and sipped my coffee,

'Will he really introduce me to his friends?'

Little Queer gave me a shrewd look.

'How many do you want to meet?'

'As many as possible darling. I want to live the life of the *real* Riviera.'

He relaxed and said, 'You'll certainly do that. By the way, living close to him can be dangerous. There've been several attempts at murder. He's lost three bodyguards and one girlfriend since I've known him. He acts the kindly old gent but he's not. He's a dangerous and erratic old bugger with many enemies. So be ready to duck at any time.'

I managed to act frightened-wide-eyed and gasping shock-horror.

'Who's after him?'

'Other gangsters and several governments, but so far he's been too clever for them.'

'*Other* gangsters? Is *he* a gangster? He seems such a lovely old dear.'

'Oh Sweetie, I've said too much. You'll have to ask him some time. If he *really* likes and trusts you he'll show off and tell you his history.'

'I'll do my best to please him.'

Although that sounded normal enough to me he again stared with a squinty-eyed knowing look as though to say, *What are you after, girl? Are you all you seem?'*

Apparently flustered, I giggled and said, 'What I mean is...I mean...you should have seen him last night. He went at me like a goat and I worried he may harm himself. And look at how exhausted he is this morning.'

'Oh Sweetie, he's done just the same with me. A night thrashing about and complete collapse at dawn – it takes him a day to recover then off we go again.'

'So could he die?'

'It's possible. But if you don't finish him off, he's likely to do it himself. He keeps Viagra and hearing aid batteries in his bedside drawer. A month ago he fumbled for the Viagra and swallowed a hearing aid battery instead.'

'Good God. What happened?'

'Well Sweetie, I don't know what it did to his insides but It certainly didn't help his erection.'

Chapter 25

My lovely Old Billionaire kept his word. Our life became a two month social whirl. He introduced Eleanor, his new American girlfriend, to dinners, soirées, high-class parties, several orgies and sex parties.

I especially enjoyed a stylish soirée attended by younger members of a Princely family. Even more I enjoyed the next night when the same members exhibited their members at a waterborne orgy on a yacht out at sea.

A couple of Princesses joined in and the night ended with exhaustion all round and no-one sure who had coupled with whom. Over a bleary breakfast on deck, in a murmur of quiet conversation, last night's cast exchanged experiences. One Princess seemed quite surprised that, in the dark, she had probably been thoroughly done over by her brother the Prince.

She slipped him a kiss and whispered, 'If it *was* you – you were wonderful.'

'Perhaps we should have another go?'

'Not if I know it's you. It wouldn't be so much fun.'

This seemed the way of things. Inside the security of their parties everyone could take any depraved sexual route with everyone else, whatever rank or relationship.

I made friends with a couple of famous young models who suggested we meet one-to-one, or if I preferred, one-to-two. We exchanged cards and when they saw Old Billionaire's address the beautiful slim teenager hissed, 'How did you manage to snare *him*?'

'We never use call girls or rent boys, Sweetie,' Little Queer told me later. 'That way brings tabloids and scandal. Like incest, we keep it all in the family.'

When un-drugged my Old Billionaire seemed a kindly sort of fellow, anxious that I enjoyed and experienced the best The Riviera could offer. But when fired up on drugs he became an explosion of carnal lust, taking on every sexual depravity singly or in groups.

Once he insisted on a threesome with Little Queer and me but became so drained and exhausted we both thought he would die. When, several nights later, he demanded a repeat, we refused, causing an enormous rage and sulk that went on for several days.

His beautiful cliff top villa – twenty gorgeous rooms, some locked and private – filled with riches of furniture and ornaments and original art by many famous old masters, demonstrated his great wealth and status.

'Is that why the house is so secure, with such high walls and razor wire and great metal security gates?' I asked Little Queer the morning he gave me a guided tour.

'There's a lot more than that,' he said. 'Come on, I'll show you.'

He unlocked two private doors, one to a room lined with screens linked to cameras showing views of approach roads, the metal gate and just about every room and corridor in the house. Even the outside terrace could be scanned from every angle.

'These cameras are great,' he said. 'They work in bright light or complete darkness,'

The second door – heavy metal and thirty centimetres thick – led down a short corridor to another, similar door, which Little Queer opened and ushered me through.

'This is his safe room in case of attack. Raiders couldn't even break in with high explosives or smoke him out, so our friend is safe from kidnap or assassination. Even if they burnt the house down he'd survive for a couple of hours on the special pure air system. After that he'd suffocate. That's why our servants never stay the night. In a case a year ago a valet opened the door to thieves then set fire to the house to cover his own tracks. The fire engines came late and discovered his poor employer roasted and suffocated in the panic room.'

He shivered.

'I hope the suffocation came first.'

'Has this house ever been attacked?'

'Twice, but we survived.'

'You were here? What happened?'

'Both times some incompetent Russian gangsters tried to get in. They managed the wall but got no further than the driveway. As soon as external security alarms sounded in the house I shoved him into the safe room and galloped back to the screen room. I watched the dumb Russians to make sure they couldn't breach the house then called for help.'

'You called the police?'

'Good God *no* Sweetie darling, what *are* you suggesting? A crowd of clumping coppers in big boots and rough uniforms is the last thing we want. They'd ruin the floors and furniture and ask too many questions. They've been trying to find an excuse to get in for years, but no, no, no. Not one gendarme has ever managed to set foot in this house.'

'So what happened?'

'In the end our three thick Russians gave up and climbed back over the wall. They didn't survive for long after. We complained to our friend The Bishop. His men tracked them down and sent them swimming in the deep blue sea a long way from here. Weighed down, of course; we like to avoid the embarrassment of evidence, especially if it floats.'

The Bishop. My God, Old Billionaire really does know The Bishop. I must be nearer than I realised.

'Who's The Bishop?'

'No more Sweetie. My lips must be sealed or they may be cut off along with the rest of my head. Stay away from such questions. Not a word to anyone.'

Head cocked to one side he held a finger to sweetly painted lips.

'Promise?' he said.

'Of course I promise. My lips are sealed too.'

He winked and said, 'Then we're both safe.'

Chapter 26

Our life together as a threesome continued happily for another few weeks.

Every so often I returned to my own villa to relax alone.

I needed time off because, working alongside Little Queer, I had settled into an exhausting routine of looking after Old Billionaire. We organised him and ourselves with the efficiency of a military operation, based on nights of crippling social activity and sex, followed by daytime rest and recovery.

During one of our few-and-far-between free evenings, relaxing after dinner on terrace with Old Billionaire, I read a newspaper report that mentioned The Bishop.

'This man sounds interesting,' I said. 'Do you know him?

'Of course I know him. A week before I met you we had dinner and discussed business. He's a terrible blackguard and an awful criminal. Completely untrustworthy and dangerous, but I like him.'

Just then Little Queer flounced onto the terrace and joined us, mumbling complaints about the servants. Old Billionaire winked at me and I smiled. No day with Little Queer is complete with some hissy little drama.

So I never asked my next question, which was, 'Will I ever meet the man?'

But at least, for now, I sat enjoying this perfect evening, so calm and warm and secure in the knowledge that my new social circle is bringing me closer to Target.

I sighed and said, 'Look at the stars and how they reflect in the sea. What beauty. How peaceful it is tonight.'

'Very poetic,' said Old Billionaire. 'Let's hope this moment of peace lasts forever.'

But it didn't.

That night we came under determined attack.

Chapter 27

Around four in the morning Little Queer scampered in and hissed, 'Armed intruders. Quick. Into the safe room.'

I jumped from bed and rushed, naked, to help Little Queer pull Old Billionaire upright and along to the safe room.

Little Queer shoved him in and tried to make me follow but I pulled back.

'I hate small spaces. I'll stay out here with you.'

'Go and get some clothes on then. I'll be in the screen room.'

He waddled away down the corridor, quite fetching in tight pink underpants.

I hurried to my private room, threw on a black gown with a large front pocket, grabbed my three miniature weapons and ran to join Little Queer.

He said, 'Pull down that big lever and cut all lights.'

'That'll make no difference,' I said, pointing at the driveway screen. 'They're wearing night-vision goggles.'

'Oh God, so they are.'

But, needing the night, I pulled this big lever and plunged the whole place into complete darkness.

Little Queer switched a different camera and zoomed in on three men moving confidently towards the main door, saying, 'They'll be lucky if they hope to break in.'

'Don't be so sure. They're professional killers, not robbers. They're dressed and tooled for murder.'

The three men, covered from head to toe in black, fully masked and carrying light machine pistols, reached the door and produced a key.

'My God, someone's set them on us. We're all dead,' whispered Little Queer.

'That depends on how well they know the house. Switch off the cameras and stay here. I'll see if I can frighten them away.'

'Don't leave me,' wailed Little Queer. 'I don't want to die alone.'

'Shut up you little fool. And let go of my arm.'

On silent bare feet I passed down the corridor to a place where our attackers must split to check different rooms. As professionals, they'd already know the layout, how many floors, and probably who slept where.

They may or may not know I am resident so Number One will certainly aim for Old Billionaire's bedroom to kill him or us both.

Number Two will head to kill Little Queer.

Probably not sure if house staff sleep in, Number Three will approach servants' quarters to eliminate witnesses.

Enough starlight filtered through windows for me work so I set up ambush at a corner in the corridor approaching Old Billionaire's bedroom.

I crouched, probably not visible as a person – more likely to be mistaken for a small piece of furniture.

Waiting, ready to spring either way, I heard the shuffle of One's soft boots approaching. The thin red line of a laser sight aimed down the corridor; meaning they were probably soldiers, not hit-men.

Good. They'll hold guns at shoulder level and swing those silly sights round at head height, concentrating only on where the dinky little red dot points.

So what use your night-vision goggles, my fine men? You're looking forwards and sideways; ignoring up and down. Any properly trained hit-man would be a different kettle of fish. These three will be easy.

Number One arrived as a tall dark shadow.

I leapt up, popped a mini-rocket into his head, caught him and his gun before they clattered to the floor and laid him down without a sound.

I then moved on tiptoe to Little Queer's room, met Number Two coming out and despatched him in the same way, catching and lowering him to the floor.

Before I found Number Three, he found me.

They must have been whispering on earpiece radios and abrupt dead silence made Three realise something had happened.

He ambushed me; stepping from the blackness of an open door and grabbing and lifting me from behind but relaxed when he felt the soft curves of a woman.

Big mistake.

Snatching the lipstick knife from my large front pocket I swung up and back, releasing the poisoned blade into his neck. This time I couldn't stop the clatter of our fall, but it didn't matter, since no one remained to come to his aid.

I stood, dusted myself down and went to find Little Queer hiding under the screens table.

'You can come out,' I said. 'It's all over.'
'What happened?'

'I went boo and they all fell down. Switch the lights on and have a look.

Chapter 28

Little Queer followed me from body to body, horror etched in his face.

I checked each one for true death.

After making sure they'd not recover I led Little Queer to the terrace and sat him down with half a glass of brandy.

I went to the balcony rail and checked the silvery night sea for any boats or ships nearby.

None, so I said, 'Come on. Drink up. We have to get rid of these bastards.'

Silent and shaking he helped me drag the three heavy men onto the terrace. Using their belts I strapped each machine gun firmly to each body and removed their pistols, knives and stun grenades from holsters.

'Now we toss this lot into the sea and no one but you and me will have any idea what happened. The guns and ammunition belts will keep them at the bottom and they'll be gone for good. And *you* will never say a *word*.'

I rolled all three bodies over twice, turning out empty pockets, checking for name tags; unzipping to reach into underclothes for laundry marks.

Nothing.

No sign of nationality or origin of men or uniforms.

Even their weapons – completely free of serial numbers or etchings – seemed manufactured for clandestine murder.

I pulled off their masks. All had exactly the same face; high cheek bones, olive skin and black eyes. They could have been brothers, or from the same tribe or clan.

Little Queer took a long swig of his brandy and found his voice.

'Who were they? Where are they from?'

'Difficult to say. They could have been Russian, Israeli, Chechen, Arab or even American.'

'Why should any of them break in here? Are they after Old Billionaire or after you?'

'Why should they be after me?'

'Because I think you're not what you seem to be.'

'Do you now.'

'What's your game?'

'All you need to know is that I'm good at it.'

'I can see that.'

'Yes. Now shut up.'

'How did a small woman like you manage to kill three armed men like that?' he quavered.

'Don't ask.'

'Why are you here?'

'Don't ask.'

'Who are you?'

'Don't ask. Shut your mouth right now and keep it shut. Make sure you tell absolutely no one what happened. Tell no one now and tell no one ever.'

'Or you'll kill me?'

'Yes. You'll follow these three over the balcony. Or worse.'

He tipped his glass to finish his brandy in one great gulp; hunched his shoulders; jumped up and flexed his arms.

'Let's get on with it then.'

We hefted each late soldier onto the rail and tipped him into his long drop.

Even in this clear and windless night, we hardly heard a splash.

Their side weapons followed. This time we made a game of it, counting the seconds each piece took to fall, splash and disappear.

Little Queer said, 'I understand you can calculate the height by the time something takes to fall.'

'You're drunk. Come on. Let's get our friend back to bed.'

We opened the panic room to find Old Billionaire curled up safe and comfortable on a bunk. Little Queer rolled back the blanket and we took him, half awake, back to bed. I rolled in alongside and kept him warm with a friendly cuddle.

Together, in comfort, we slept until mid morning.

Chapter 29

We woke and ate brunch on the terrace. Just Old Billionaire and me. Little Queer kept out of the way.

Old Billionaire, deep in thought, took great care and concentration in buttering his croissant, spreading jam and making certain he poured exactly the right amount of warm milk into his coffee.

I stayed quiet, taking equal care with my breakfast.

After a while, he brushed crumbs from his lap, leaned back and said, 'What happened last night?'

'Nothing. Only a couple of dumb goons who managed to get over the wall. They never made it into the house. After ten minutes they gave up and left.'

'For some reason I became very confused but remember you pushing me into the panic room. I remember you refused to join me. Why?'

'I don't like being confined.'

He gave me a look that said, *I don't believe a word,* and smiled with a slight shake of his head.

That afternoon Little Queer sidled up and whispered, 'He's been checking round and knows something happened. He got to the security tapes before I could delete evidence of your little game. He saw those guys using a key to open the door. And he may have seen some blood on the terrace.'

For the next two days Old Billionaire stayed off drugs and alcohol and remained deep in thought, hardly speaking to me or Little Queer, and at night, he banished me to my own bedroom.

On the third day he sent Little Queer out on an errand and said to me, 'Something happened that night that you are not telling me. Somehow you scared those raiders off. What did you do?'

I shrugged. 'I think they were surprised to have a little naked woman screaming at them.'

'Did they get in? I saw on the security tape that they had a key.'

'I can't remember. It all happened so fast.'

'You told Little Queer to close down the cameras. Why?'

'I don't remember doing that. Perhaps *he* did it to save worrying you.'

Old Billionaire raised an eyebrow and murmured. 'Oh come on. You did *something*. I don't know what but it must have been effective.'

I shrugged again.

'And it must have been frightening. I've noticed that since the incident, Little Queer is more respectful of you. For instance, he doesn't call you Sweetie anymore.'

'What do you expect me to say? I don't know what Little Queer told you and I don't know what you are talking about.'

'Well, my dear girl. Little Queer has so far said nothing. But I think I am mysteriously in your debt in a way I'll never know. Will you ever tell me?'

I peeped at him over the rim of my coffee cup.

'Ah. I see the answer is no. But I thank you for whatever you did to save me.'

I blew him a kiss.

He chuckled and said, 'You may or may not know that I am a financier of many world-wide deals. Some things I finance are not popular with certain political groups or countries so I run risks a normal financier would never need to guard against.'

'Risks serious enough to get you killed?'

'It's been tried before but – by amazing luck - always failed. Some unseen guardian angel hovering nearby saved me each time.'

'You're lucky.'

'Yes. But this time my guardian angel is in full view and living in my house. Did someone employ *you* as my guardian angel?'

'What an odd idea.'

This time he laughed out loud.

'I see you'll never confess. I like to think that one of my friends or colleagues hired you. If so I'll find out and thank him – or her – and make sure you get a big bonus.'

'Oh God, what a story. I'm just a simple everyday rich American heiress looking for fun and a husband. A young man if you don't mind. So can we cut the crap and have a normal conversation?'

'Very well – Let's change the subject. Can you sing?'

'Yes. I'm a sort of contralto. They thought me good enough at university to sing in both opera and choirs at university. Why?'

'I've invited a special friend to dinner tomorrow night. He likes opera. Little Queer is a good pianist so during dinner can you perform an aria or two?'

'It will be a pleasure.'

'Good. My friend and I have important private business to discuss so you won't join us for dinner or drinks. You'll just come in, sing and leave. Does that offend you?'

'Of course not. But my voice is rusty. I haven't practised for a while. I'll need a tuning fork set in E.'
'I'll send Little Queer out to buy one immediately.'

Chapter 30

'Who's coming?' I asked Little Queer.

'I don't know.'

'Did you give Old Billionaire any detail of the other night?'

'I wouldn't dare.'

'Well he's noticed something's changed because you're no longer calling me Sweetie.'

'Alright. I wouldn't dare, *Sweetie*.'

'Get back to how you were with me or we'll be in trouble. And, for God's sake, cheer up.'

'Why don't you come tuning-fork shopping with me? That'll show how friendly we are.'

'Good idea.'

So off we went, me dressed to kill in the way of any right thinking rich American heiress; Little Queer in flowing multi-coloured beach shirt and extra tight pink shorts.

I laughed and said, 'You're showing off too much swinging arse, little man.'

He giggled and said, 'And *you* are showing off too much swinging tit, Sweetie.'

He took my arm and, once again friends, we went to buy the most expensive fine steel tuning-fork in Monaco then sat in a classy café sipping coffee, eating cream cakes and making bitchy remarks about the passing parade.

Back at the villa we practised; Little Queer on the piano, me trying to sing. I needed a gargle and several twangs of the tuning-fork to get near pitch. Little Queer turned out to be an intuitive pianist and musician, able to direct me to better voice, especially at high levels.

'Maria Callas you'll never be, Sweetie, but you're fine for an intimate dinner party.'

Luckily we knew the same operas quite well and after a few goes had four or five arias pretty well sewn up.

'You'll be a hit, Sweetie. I promise. You'll be a big hit.'

'Do you think so?

'Yes. Especially if you remember; low dress, big breaths and plenty of tit. The singing won't matter then.

I threatened him with the sharp end of my tuning-fork. He cowered back in mock fear just as Old Billionaire came into the room.

'Happy to see you're all relaxed again after our shock of the other night. My goodness, I can see we're in for a great performance.'

'I hope he just means the music,' whispered Little Queer.

The next evening, sitting with Little Queer in the screens room I watched three large cars sweep in. Old Billionaire stood by the door, waiting to greet his guest.

'This must be a *real* Mr Important,' said Little Queer. 'He'll be a prince or sheikh or ambassador or arms dealer or drugs baron; they all need him. But he only meets the *really* important ones outside by the door.''

'Does Old Billionaire deal in arms and drugs?'

'He doesn't *deal*. Not directly. He makes and finances deals – brings people together and puts up the money. All the baddies in the world trust him, Sweetie. And all the governments in the world hate him. That's why he's so dangerous to be near. One day he'll be assassinated. Bang. Just like that. And one of us could easily go with him.'

'Why do you stay then?'

'Wish I had somewhere else to go, Sweetie.'

Large men jumped from the cars and ushered Mr Important forward to be hugged and welcomed by Old Billionaire. The cars then set up a half circle across the gate – 'In case other baddies try to bust in,' – said Little Queer.

An hour later, after they'd eaten, we did our musical turn. I couldn't quite see Mr Important, hunched down in a high wing chair but I did notice a kindly smile and twinkling eyes when he lifted his arms to applaud.

All through my performance he kept peeking round the chair-wing in quick little head-bobs – 'Giving you the once-over, Sweetie' – whispered Little Queer.

Our act over, we were ushered from the room and then out of the house with all the cooks and staff in for the event.

I went in one car with three heavies to a swank hotel room with telephone cut off and strict instructions not to go into the corridor or speak to anyone and imagined Little Queer in the same situation. Food or drink I ordered through a brooding heavy sitting outside my door.

So this is how the top criminal fraternity live.

Luxury and fear with stifling security and their women kept in check.

I'm learning all the time it is not easy getting into position to kill one of these arrogant bastards.

Chapter 31

Next day, released and back at the house I cornered Little Queer. He looked pretty exhausted.

'Did they lock you up for the night too?'

'Yes. And oh, Sweetie, what a wonderful time I had. My guard – a lovely hunk –as queer as queer can be. We fell in love straight away.'

'So what happened?'

'What do you think? He had all sorts of equipment and substances to help the night go round. And round, and round and round. In fact this room is going round right now, darling.'

'So you fell on your feet.'

'More on my front, Sweetie, but that's none of your business.'

He giggled.

'But along with all the sex, drugs and drink I *did* find out one bit of gossip you'll never believe. What do you think of *this?* Our guest last night was...that awful criminal known as The *Bishop*.'

'What?'

I clenched fists and teeth in almighty effort to keep control.

Shit. We were in the same room and I didn't know.

Little Queer prattled on; 'Yes, Sweetie. We've actually *seen* the man no one *ever* sees. He looked a harmless old dear, don't you think?'

'What I think right now is that you look ill and awful enough bugger off to bed and recover. I'm exhausted too, so that's where I'm going.'

'You're right. I do feel awful. Every little noise, including your voice, is going right through my head.'

'Serves you right.'

'Yes. It does. So please don't speak until at least tomorrow morning.'

We parted.

In my private room I paced from wall to wall, quivering with rage.

Shit. Shit. Shit. I could have got him there and then. Shit and shit again.

I growled and grumped for five minutes then calmed down enough to argue the case with my image in the mirror.

'But think, you fool. If you'd known he'd be there and planned a Hit, you'd have had to kill Old Billionaire and Little Queer at the same time. And all the heavies. What about them? Use your head.'

'Yes. Yes. You're right. And I'd never have got away, would I?'

'Of course not. But you've moved ahead to an advantage in this game. You now know exactly what he looks like and I can tell he fancied you like mad. Hardly took his eyes off you.'

'Again, you're right.'

'So there you have a way to get alongside for your Hit. Find a way of meeting him again. Wheedle your way into his circle and perhaps his bed.'

'Thanks. Good advice. I feel better already.'

Chapter 32

Old Billionaire called me to his secure office and said, 'My important visitor enjoyed your performance very much. He found you attractive in every way and asked to be introduced but I refused.'

'Why?'

'He leads a strange life with a wife and three mistresses all living together. I told him he didn't want another mistress, especially one as naive and inexperienced as you.'

'Me? Naive and inexperienced?'

We both laughed at the thought.

'What did he say?'

'He laughed too and didn't believe a word. But whatever he offers – stay away. Don't be fooled by the cuddly little old man act. He is bad and dangerous.'

'What's his name?'

'No one knows.'

I asked no more, content that I'd been noticed and would almost certainly be welcomed into The Bishop's household when the chance came.

For the next month we settled to a quiet life around the villa, while Old Billionaire worked in his office from dawn to dusk.

He stayed off booze and drugs and told me to sleep in my own room for the time being. 'I'm too busy for games just now. Sorry but you'll just have to put up with it. Go out and find entertainment if you wish. A couple of men or a couple of women if that suits you. I won't mind.'

But I didn't. I wanted to remain untainted in his eyes and, anyway, for a couple of weeks I enjoyed the rest;

using the gym and swimming pool several hours a day to keep strength and reactions in trim.

By middle of the third week, the effort to remain untainted began to wear off.

I said to Little Queer, 'I'm getting bored. How long does this go on?'

'It's always like it when he's working on a big deal. He's always extra careful when it's The Bishop. Get it wrong and you get killed.'

Old Billionaire's work included many meetings. Little Queer and I would keep out of the way but watch them come and go from the screens room.

We saw Arabs in fluttering robes and headdress, sharp suited accountants with fancy briefcases and a variety of obvious gangsters of every complexion from Mexican dark to Columbian smooth. We even tabbed a few American heavies in floral shirts and Bermuda shorts.

'Devils every one,' hissed Little Queer.

For each visit I kept my mini-rocket pistol strapped with masking tape under my left armpit. I knew that if things turned ugly, these people would expect to kill Old Billionaire and everyone in the house.

During the fourth week Old Billionaire began to emerge from his office for a short break every couple of hours, looking drained and exhausted.

'My poor dear man,' whispered Little Queer. 'I wish we could help.'

'Nothing we can do,' I said. 'We'll make sure he recovers when it's over.'

One afternoon I went shopping and returned to find Old Billionaire dead.

Chapter 33

Little Queer met me in a state of absolute fear. He dragged me into his arms, sobbing and shaking.

'He's gone,' he howled. 'We've lost him.'

'For God's sake let me go. Lost who?'

'Old Billionaire. He died ten minutes ago. Came from his office and keeled over on the terrace. Come and look. You may be able to do something.'

Old Billionaire lay flat on his back, mouth open; trails of dried dribble snaking down his chin.

I tested.

'Dead as a doornail,' I said. 'Who do we call? The coroner? The mayor? The police?'

Little Queer threw himself into a big soft chair, hands over his face, sobbing.

'None of those,' he wept. 'Government people are last thing we want.'

I ignored him and called the police. Within an hour a couple of solemn officials arrived and took over, murmuring instructions to each other. They double-checked Old Billionaire had really and truly left us and made three or four quiet telephone calls.

'Please leave everything to us now, Madame. We'll look after your husband and make all arrangements.'

In no time at all they efficiently arranged an undertaker, efficiently supervised removal of the body and efficiently whispered polite advice.

'You may wish to remove yourselves from these premises for the time being. Other people may have an interest in what went on here and come to clean up. Be gone at least two days. After that we'll give you details of the funeral and will.'

Little Queer and I packed and left immediately.

'Where are we going?' he asked.

'I've just the place,' I said and marched him to a bus stop on the route past my villa in the hills behind Nice.

'By bus? By *bus*? I've never been on a *bus* in my life.'

'Use your head. The people coming to clean up may want to clean us up too. We go by bus and they don't know where we've gone.'

'Good thinking. Come on then. Let's get away from here.'

Settled in my villa – 'Nice place, Sweetie,' – we discussed whether our two solemn officials were from the coroner or the criminal fixers.

'They'll be fixers, Sweetie. It'll all be nice and official in the end but for the moment we keep out of it. Heads down is best if we don't want to have the damned things hacked off.'

On the third day we returned – by bus – to Old Billionaire's mansion in Monaco and found it tidy, clean and completely cleared of all documents and files. They'd turned Old Billionaire's office into an elderly gentleman's study; a kind of intellectual smoking room for the retired businessman. And very good it looked

We hung around for three days, wary and unsure of what to do.

Chapter 34

Our day staff came and went as normal, arriving early morning and leaving after serving dinner.

No change there.

But Little Queer took fright at the sight of two heavies leaning on a car parked across the road from our gate, staring at our house and occasionally wandering up to the gate and peering in.

'They've been doing that for three hours. They're watching us for some reason. Don't open the door and stay away from windows until I work out what they're up to.'

In the end he took his small store of courage in hand and minced out for a chat, returning in a state of high excitement.

'They're here to look after us and one is my special friend from the other night. Do you think I can have him in for a cuddle when his shift finishes?'

'You can have him in for a cuddle anywhere you like except here. And what shift?'

He pouted and sulked for a moment.

'Never mind. I'll be able to see him later. He says that until the boss is sure no baddies are planning to break in and cause trouble - such as kill you and me – his men will mount twenty-four hour guard over us.'

'Good. Are we allowed out?'

'Yes. Whenever we want. So when he's off duty I'll be able to mount a four-hour session with my personal guard. Do you know anywhere safe we can mount in private?'

'If you're thinking of my villa, the answer's a big fat no. That's one place we're safe. It's our absolutely secret bolthole and stays that way.'

He pouted again and threw another sulk.

'Make sure you keep to the sea-facing side of the house,' I said. 'Your friend wouldn't be able to guard us against a sniper on the roof of one of those buildings opposite.'

'Oh you're so *professional*,' sniggered my Little Queer with an arched eyebrow. 'Where *did* you learn it all?'

So we closed the curtains and tiptoed round, leading a very careful life for a week.

Then came the next shock.

Chapter 35

On a bright clear morning our two solemn officials returned.

'We've made arrangements for the funeral,' said Solemn Official One.

'And we have a Will that may feature you both,' said Solemn Official Two.

'What do you mean *may*?' lisped Little Queer. 'Are we in it or not?'

'Wait till after the interment in two days time.'

Shaken by this news, we stood behind the curtains and watched them leave.

'We're in the Will,' gasped Little Queer. 'What has he left us?'

'I can see why you're in it, by why me?'

'Gratitude. He knew you saved his life.'

'Not for long.'

The funeral, held in a medieval mountain village, showed how important Old Billionaire and his business skills must have been to successful men from various areas; political, criminal, financial, drugs, arms, prostitution.

There may even have been a few honest citizens available to see him off.

But not many.

Old Billionaire would probably have enjoyed this sort of baffling religious service; a mixture of Christian, Jewish and Eastern Orthodox.

"It's always like this,' whispered Little Queer. 'No one knows where any of these guys come from. So they use a mish-mash of religions in the hope they send them off in the right direction.'

Afterwards, a parade of expensive automobiles wound down the mountain road to a large beach hotel and a surprisingly jolly wake. Floods of beautiful women joined in the eating, drinking and dancing and general debauchery.

'Is The Bishop here?' I whispered to Little Queer.

Before he could reply I turned to a tap on my shoulder and looked straight into the eyes of my own personal Chessman, last seen outside the football stadium in Nice.

He stared at me.

I stared back and edged a hand into my bag to grip my tiny pistol. A perfect place to kill and walk away. No one would notice.

He smiled.

'You and your friend must come with me.'

'Why?'

'The Will is about to be read. You are both mentioned. I've been sent to bring you.'

Chapter 36

The silly old bugger left Little Queer five million dollars and me three million.

Three million?

'Why?'

'Without you, he'd have had a horrible death,' said Little Queer.

'I don't deserve it.'

'Well, you can't give it back now, can you?'

We left the lawyer's room to find my Chessman waiting outside.

'You must come with me again, Madame. Not you, young man. Just the lady.'

'Why?'

'My friend wishes to meet you,'

'Oh God. Not another one. Does any man in France pick up a woman for himself? Do they all need to send a messenger?'

He threw his head back and laughed. His slicked-back hair shone. His too-white teeth glistened.

'Not a man, my little American. This time it's a woman. My employer's wife. She's heard of you and wants to meet.'

'That's a bit different,' I said and winked at Little Queer. 'See you later darling.'

Ushering me back to the wake and through the throng of happy mourners, he managed twice to rub a palm across my buttocks, the second time, whispering, 'When she's finished with you, perhaps we can meet.'

'Why? What have you got to interest me?'

'I won't tell you now, but it's worth seeing.'

'Ho-ho,' I said, grasping his exploring fingers and directing them under and onto my quim, where he stroked and tickled.

I shivered and whispered, 'Yes, perhaps it might be fun if meet.'

Like all gullible men, he fell for it.

'Good. I promise it will be more fun than you can ever imagine.'

A young woman perched on a tall bar stool; tall, slim, long blonde hair in a cascade over her shoulders; thin elegant face and bright eyes; a tight dress and no obvious underclothes.

Must be a model.

No. Not skinny enough.

'My husband heard you sing a short time ago. He spoke of you and wants to meet again. But I check you out first.'

My God. Could I be luckier?

'What makes you think I want to meet him? Or be checked out by you?'

With an up-and-back sweep of her hands, she lifted and dropped her mane of hair in a flowing wave.

Quite graceful. Perhaps a dancer.

With a most beautiful smile she said, 'You'll find I make the checking really, *really* enjoyable. And you'll find meeting my husband really, *really* rewarding. If I think he'll like you.'

'You're his pimp?'

'I suppose I am. But I'm my own pimp too.'

'Let's get to it then Madame Pimp. Let's get checking.'

Chapter 37

'We'll go to my gym,' she said.

Less of a gym; more of an all-female brothel full of absolutely beautiful women lounging around luxury open rooms and being attended in every possible way by other absolutely beautiful women or – heaven help us – by big butch dykes, all short-cropped hair and muscles and skimpy leather bikinis.

'My God, you could have a great time here,' I said.

'That's the idea. Come on. I've reserved a private room.'

The room – an enormous bed, a massage couch, a large square bath, a side table laden with oils, perfumes, soaps and walls lined with handcuffs, chains, ropes – seemed set up for whatever pleasure a kinky girl might require or request.

The Bishop's wife wriggled from her expensive dress threw it aside and pulled me into a violent embrace, sliding perfect breasts across the silk material of my dress until her nipples stood proud.

'Look at what you do to me,' she gasped.

Gripping my thigh between hers, she took hold of my buttocks and pulled me in and with the sinuous sway of a practiced dancer, rubbed herself up and down, thrusting with such force I staggered and nearly fell.

I pushed back, tipped her onto the bed and dragged off my clothes then fell upon her, kissing, licking, fondling, whispering; asking what she wanted.

'Everything, darling. *Everything*. Make me come again and again.'

So I did. On the bed, on the floor, on the massage couch – oil everywhere – and when, exhausted, she begged me to stop I continued for another ten minutes.

We ended up sitting at opposite ends of the bath – water perfumed and not too hot – soaping and stroking. I edged my big toe into her quim and wiggled. She lay back and sighed, eyes closed, long hair hanging in damp sweat-and-soap strands, flicking her hips against the pressure.

'What imagination, darling. What *wonderful* imagination. Where did you learn all these tricks?'

I giggled.

'Round and about,' I said.

'In America?'

'Some. And in China, and Japan, and Brazil and lots of interesting places, it all comes from the benefit of travel.'

'Did you ever work as a prostitute?'

'Oh yes. In several countries. Just for the experience, you understand.'

'I'd love to do that.'

'Why don't you?'

'He'd kill me. I can have as many women as I like but no men. Ever. It's not fair.'

'He's jealous?'

'Possessive. He's possessive with us all. He has three other women, you know. If you're not careful he'll pull you into his menagerie.'

'Is that why you're checking me out?'

'Probably.'

'So what happens next?'

'We dry and dress and I'll get a couple of butch hairdressers in to tidy us up, if you like. They get up to all sorts of interesting tricks.'

'Normal hairdressers will do thanks.'

'Then we have coffee and a chat and I report back.'

'A good report?'

'Probably.'

Chapter 38

We dried, dressed and went to an expensive oak panelled tea room designed for the very rich; antique furniture and private booths all round the walls.

'We'll hide in that one near the back,' she said and, as soon as we were in, embraced me with an enormous wet kiss, all tongue and thrusting hips.

'What was that for?'

'I may be in love. I think I'll keep you for myself. Bugger my husband.'

'Did I pass then, Madame Pimp?'

'Flying colours.'

'Do you always do this?'

'Only in special cases.'

'Why am I special?'

'He's nervous of new women at the moment. His work brings jealousy and danger and he had reports of a woman in Paris asking about him. And he heard that a woman may have murdered one of his associates – an Arab – in a clever way. So he is extra careful although you came with good recommendations from Old Billionaire.'

We finished our coffee and kissed goodbye.

Back at Old Billionaire's villa I found Little Queer in a high state of worry.

'Our two solemn friends are coming to see us. They're bringing our cheques and some news.'

'What news?'

'Well, I don't know yet, do I? But every time they visit the news is bad.'

An hour later they turned up.

'Why don't they ever smile?' whispered Little Queer.

We sat with them in Old Billionaire's study. Without a flicker of emotion they handed over our inheritance from Old Billionaire in two negotiable money orders.

'Sign here please. Then immediately leave this house and never come back.'

Little Queer burst into tears.

'Leave Immediately?

'Yes.'

'How,' wailed Little Queer. 'This is Old Billionaire's villa. I've lived here for years.'

'This house is owned by a corporation and you must leave immediately.'

I said, 'Ridiculous. We will not. We need a couple of days.'

'Very well. We'll authorise forty-eight hours from precisely now. At the same time in two days our own bailiffs will arrive. They may be quite rough in ejecting you.'

'How, by throwing us off the veranda?' sniffed Little Queer.

'Possibly. They can be very definite.'

They left and Little Queer turned on me; hissing, 'You saved us from three armed gorillas, so why couldn't you save us from those two dodos?'

'Don't be stupid. Those gorillas could have been sent by anyone from anywhere in the world. These guys are sent from just across the road by people we probably met at the funeral. They can't know about the gorillas or we'd have had another killing visit by now.'

Later that afternoon The Bishop's wife called.

'I hear you're being evicted.'

'By your husband?'

'I think so. Let me know where you end up so we can meet for another session. And my husband wants you to come and sing for him.'

'I'd love to.'

At last. Target in plain sight.

Chapter 39

Late that same evening I insisted we go immediately and took Little Queer by bus to my villa.

'What's the rush? We still have two days. And why are we leaving most of our things? And why are we going in the dark'

'Use your head. They'll think we'll take forty-eight hours to pack then watch and follow. We need security. Slip away now and they'll not see us go. Bring only what fits in your pocket. Now you're a millionaire you can replace everything in a week, without even noticing.'

Next morning, sitting in shade by the pool I spent several hours planning my next moves.

It seems that Eleanor the musician has found her way in.

Now Maddy the Assassin must complete The Hit and find her way out.

A few weeks ago Old Billionaire told me that The Bishop's house is amazingly secure and guarded by a group of ever-changing ruthless international killers backed by the latest electronic security systems.

'What's he frightened of?' I asked.

'Half the criminal world and most major governments want him dead, one way or another. They'd pay a lot to have it done. So he pays a great deal more and shuffles guards every few weeks so none can be bought. And he upgrades electronics systems every couple of months making it impossible for even the cleverest hacker to break in.'

'So he leaves nothing to chance.'

'Exactly. One day a killer may get through but having struck will never get out alive. It's a suicide mission.'

Sitting under my beautiful orange bougainvillea, a plan began to form in my head.

Now I'm invited in half my job is done.

Now for the second half – The Hit and Escape.

After a couple of hours I had it all worked out.

Chapter 40

First I advised Little Queer to get his millions into a bank.

'Do it now. No delay. For all we know they'll cancel the cheques when they find we've disappeared.'

He rushed to dress in reasonably sober colours and hurried off.

When he had gone I did the same. My bank showed no surprise at such a large deposit, not even a raised eyebrow. I suppose three million dollars equals petty cash in Monaco.

I visited four department stores and bought several mid-range outfits; the type worn by a normal housewife.

Then to the smooth lawyer who'd helped me buy my villa. He too showed no surprise when I bustled in with a pile of shopping bags and signed the property over to Little Queer.

'You did *what*?' squeaked Little Queer. 'You've given me this *house*? Why?'

'Because what I do next may be dangerous for you, so stay out of sight for a while. No one knows about this place. Keep your mouth shut and your head down and live here alone for at least six months.'

'I know what you're going to do. I know what you are.'

'Don't say another word – to me or anyone else.'

I kissed the top of his head.

'In ten minutes I'll be gone. We'll never meet again so forget me completely along with anything you saw and any suspicions you have about me.'

I swear he blinked away a tear.

Thirty minutes later Eleanor booked in to the grandest and most expensive hotel in Nice and called The Bishop's wife. She burst through my door wearing nothing but a silk dress. She pulled up my gown and dived into an hour of frantic sex.

Exhausted, we fell apart and lay on the bed, stroking and touching everywhere damp, soft and intimate.

'What was that all about?' I whispered.

'Darling. This is our last session. Once you're in the family we are finished. My husband likes to have four women available, me and three others. I'm the wife and official. The others are toys and removable. We can get it off with him and no one else. As I told you he's very possessive.'

'Why four?'

'Status. He's showing his power. We lost one of our toys a few months ago and he's been looking for a replacement ever since. I think you may be it.'

'Lost one how?'

'He had her killed. It's boring being one of his women. We're in a harem - all we do is hang around waiting for him to show us some attention. For a bit of excitement she started fucking one of his Chessmen so he topped them both – cut off her tits and his balls and threw the lot in the sea.'

'Just because they fucked?'

'No, they fell in love and wanted to get out so offered to testify against him. Big mistake. Once you're in there's no way out. You're his for life.'

'So you think he expects me to join as number four?'

Sure. He wouldn't be giving you the once-over for any other reason.'

'Is he any good in bed?'

'Useless. Gets it up. Gets it in. Gets it out. That's it. Finito. No pleasure for me. No pleasure for anyone. He's a dead duck in the fucking department.'

'So what happens next?'

'I came here to warn you. Now I go back and tell him where you are. Sometime in the next few days you'll be summoned to sing. And to dance. And to service him in every way he can think of. If he likes what you do you're in. You join the family and lose a life. Don't say I didn't warn you.'

'Thanks. I'll think it over,'

She wept as she left.

'I've fallen in love,' she said.

We kissed. I pretended to weep with her.

'Me too,' I lied.

Later that afternoon, dressed as a prim little housewife, I went by train to one of the big Italian coastal towns, found a recording studio and commissioned two sessions.

'And I need a pianist,' I said.

'We have one of the best in Italy. He'll help you through the difficult bits.'

Next morning I made two discs; on the first I sang arias with piano backing, on the second my pianist played the same arias alone.

I returned to Nice and waited three days before my summons came.

Chapter 41

The call came. I recognised the voice – my own personal Chessman.

'I'll be with you in fifteen minutes. Don't dress yet. I'll tell you what to wear when I get there.'

I made certain personal preparations and waited on the balcony, wearing only my gown.

He entered my room.

No change from the first time I saw him; silly little pencil moustache; shiny greased-back hair; arrogant grin.

He looked me up and down. 'What a dolly. I could do with a bit of you myself. Perhaps after your interview.'

'Perhaps. We'll see. But for now, what am I supposed to wear?'

'A blue dress and nothing else.'

'Why blue?'

'His favourite colour. What Boss wants, Boss gets. Boss wants blue then blue it is.

'And nothing else?'

'Only shoes.'

He followed me to the bedroom and watched me strip from my gown and, naked but for sexy silver high heels, move round the room, selecting and laying several blue dresses on the bed.

Making sure he saw plenty of tight arse and swinging tits by bending to caress the material and turning to look over my shoulder, I asked which he liked best.

'All of it. Every bit. What a show. We'll do it again later. But for now, hurry, or The Boss will think I'm getting some before he has a chance.'

I laid out a flowing royal blue with swirly skirt and top clinging enough to give a hint of nipple.

'Wow,' he said. 'What an act.'

'All for you,' I said with tipped head and sweet smile.

The act certainly made sure he didn't look too closely at my face or profile and, perhaps, connect me to Dominique.

I gave him a little more entertainment by sitting straight-backed before my mirror, applying makeup and fixing my hair with raised arms.

As expected, he couldn't resist the offer, slipping his hands under my armpits and fondling my tits. I giggled and let him have a feel but tapped a hand a straying south towards my bush with the teeth of my comb.

'After the interview,' I whispered. 'We agreed, after the interview.'

'Damn. I'll just have to accept seconds.'

I pushed him away, pulled on my blue dress and did a twirl.

'How do I look?'

'Drop-dead gorgeous. Any man would die for you.'

I laughed.

'Come on then. Let's get going.'

Chapter 42

I picked up my tiny jewelled handbag.

His face changed to hard and brutal.

He snatched the bag and threw it across the room.

'I said nothing else. A blue dress and shoes. *Nothing else.*'

'But darling. I must have my bag. Makeup, wipes, a couple of records, my tuning fork.'

'Your *what*?'

'My tuning fork. Look.'

I retrieved the bag and showed him.

'There. Empty it and see for yourself. Your Boss has asked me to sing. Look.'

He tipped the bag out.

'I need the tuning fork to find the right note. I need the makeup and wipes to repair my face after the interview. One record is piano backing for when I sing, the other is a recording of the arias he likes. I'll leave it as a present.'

He frowned, obviously baffled but persuaded.

'Ok. You can take it. But security will check it at the castle.'

'The castle? We're going to a castle?'

'You bet. High walls and heavy gates. How do you think The Boss has remained alive so long?'

'Is it difficult to get in and get out?'

'Sure is. Everyone is logged both ways and checked for weapons. So if you're carrying a gun better leave it here or they'll shoot you as soon as they see it.'

He laughed at the thought of this little half-naked woman hiding a gun in her skimpy clothes and gave me back my bag.

At the castle gate two enthusiastic gorillas– big men all muscle and probing fingers – gave me a detailed body search taking their time to feel me all over, including armpits and quim. I shivered with the beginnings of pleasure at their expert touch.

'That was fun. Do you do it again when I leave?'

They laughed.

'Not if you're with him.'

They held up my bag. Chessman said, 'Nothing in there. I've already checked.'

I could see that these guys were professionals – apart from losing concentration while stroking and feeling a beautiful taut body from head to toe.

Chessman drove me through a small estate to a car park alongside an enormous brownstone building, all turrets and lead lined windows.

'So it really is a castle,' I said, looking around in apparent awe, while checking exits, entrances and where guards stood or patrolled. 'Why so many guards?'

'The Boss likes them to be seen. He wants you to be scared. As I said, this is how he makes sure he stays alive.'

'It must be a strange way to live.'

'You may think so but we're used to it.'

'So what happens when my interview finishes?'

'I'll be waiting here with the car. We drive out together. I take you to my pad and we play lots of special games together. That's the way it is. So be ready.'

I took a deep breath and a firm grip on my handbag. Trotting up the steps I entered The Bishop's den.

Chapter 43

A tough looking Chinese servant dressed in white welcomed me with a bow and ushered me through an impressive hall to a wide staircase.

I turned and waved at my Chessman. He raised a thumb and said, 'Be good. That Chink is fluent in four martial arts and can kill with one finger.'

I showed a middle finger in reply.

Chessman laughed and called, 'See you later.'

Chinaman led me up the stairs and along two corridors. I counted the number of footsteps from stairs to large blue door that Chinaman opened.

He stood back and bowed me through into a large room beautifully furnished in varying shades of blue with a deep lush carpet, expensive soft chairs and sofa, a large desk and a luxury divan the size of a double bed. And in the corner, thank God, a large music system. Perfect for my two discs.

A room wide floor-to-ceiling window looked down a steep cliff and across stunning mountain scenery sloping down to azure sea shining in the distance.

No chance of being spied on from outside.

I wandered round from door to window as though in admiration, trailing my fingers along smooth oak panelled walls, checking for cameras or secret access, but found none.

This room, with only one door to guard, had been designed for complete privacy.

Anything could happen here, business, seduction – even murder – and remain completely private.

Clever old Bishop.

Standing erect by the window, shoulders back, tits out, I waited, pretending to be absorbed by the view. I knew the sunlight filtering through my almost transparent dress gave a sex show he'd be unable to ignore, with first advantage to me.

I heard a swish as the almost silent door opened.

Reflected in the window I saw The Bishop slip in on bare feet. He turned and locked the door, keeping an eye on me over his shoulder.

He popped the key in a pocket of his long blue robe and said, 'Amazing view, isn't it?'

I half-turned to reply and saw him transfixed.

'Don't move,' he snapped. 'I'm busy studying my own view from here.'

I gave a girlish giggle and remained in my half-turn, showing off my perfect curve from hip to slightly wiggling breast. It's marvellous the tit-wiggle a giggle will give when needed.

'Turn now, but slowly.'

I did as ordered, making sure he saw everything on offer as a vague shadow but clear enough to entice. I opened my arms to lift my tits and remained at a slight half-angle to show my well-brushed puff of pubic bush outlined by the sunlight.

He sighed and said, 'Lovely. And all in blue.'

In my best American accent, I whispered, 'Yes, darling. What's with the blue?'

He shrugged.

'I just like blue.'

We stood looking at each other, studying and confirming. I remembered the kindly face and twinkling eyes but not how short he looked.

'You're beautiful,' he said.

'Yes. But only what you see on the outside. Inside I'm real dirty – as dirty you want.'

He chuckled.

'We've met before,' he said.

'Not really. You were sitting. I don't think you could see me properly.'

'I saw enough.'

'Good.'

He asked, 'Do you smoke?'

'No.'

'Drugs?'

'No.'

'Do you drink?'

'No.'

'What *do* you do wrong?'

I giggled.

'That's for you to find out.'

'Ok. But for now, I think you are here to sing for me.'

'Yes.'

'Well. Let's get on with it. You sing and I'll listen. Then when I'm ready we'll make beautiful music together.'

I said, 'Sure. But I'll put my backing on first.'

He watched my every move to the music system, probably hoping a tit would fall out when I leaned forward to set the disc.

I now had him absolutely mesmerised. With all his concentration on sex and me, he had no defence against what would happen next. As I said to Journalist all those weeks ago – it's easier for a woman to get close.

He stiffened as I reach into my bag, but relaxed when I brought out and tapped the tuning fork. I hummed a couple of times to reach pitch and started the music. The lovely opening notes of the first aria rang from speakers all round the room.

I turned up the sound, tiptoed as though on stage to the centre of the room and began to sing.

It went well. He settled on a large sofa and crossed his legs, leaning back in obvious bliss, relaxed and softened by the sound and sight of this woman singing his favourite music whilst slowly swaying in a gentle display of inviting sexuality.

This man will be easy to kill.

Today I seemed in fine voice and soared through several practice stanzas before settling to sing in fine style through two short pieces, followed by a long aria.

Overcome by appreciation, his eyes closed and his head fell back.

I moved nearer.

He must ave sensed the change. His head snapped up, his eyes opened sharp and wary, the twinkling eyes turned vicious.

I pretended not to notice and shifted position several times so he could see the natural movement of an artiste in full flow. He settled again into the relaxed kindly man appreciating music and a beautiful woman.

Near the end of the long aria he stood and said, 'Enough singing. I'm ready for sex. Come here.'

'Wait,' I said. 'We'll do it to music.'

I switched discs, found the second aria and turned the sound up further. My recorded voice soared through the room.

'There. This is the best way to fuck.'

I turned back.

He lifted his robe, and presented a huge erect cock, saying, 'Alright then girl. If you like doing it to music come and play my flute.'

I knelt and gave him a quick blow – quick because he seemed to have no staying power.

He nearly gave me a mouthful but I jerked back and let it fly over the carpet.

'Oops,' I said and giggled.'

His face changed to blazing fury and he started to beat me around the head. I lifted my arms in protection and he knocked me down. Rolling me over he produced a whip, pulled up my dress and started stinging my bare buttocks with expert strokes, enough to hurt but not to mark.

I'd never had this before, but let him carry on. I didn't enjoy it but I knew how this little episode would end and he didn't

'Do you like this?' he hissed.

'Love it, darling.'

'Then stand up and bend over.'

'But first a hug,' I cried. 'Give me a hug.'

He hauled me upright and held me tight.

I threw my arms around him and scratched the sharp prongs of my tuning fork along the back of his neck.

The poison acted in three seconds.

With a sigh he collapsed. I held and lowered him to the floor.

Job done.

I took wipes from my bag and applied more poison to the tuning-fork. May need it later.

Now. Howdo I get out of here?

At that moment the door opened and in walked his wife.

Chapter 44

She stopped, rigid with shock.

'How the hell did you get in here?' I snarled.

'What's happened?' she squeaked.

'He died. Just fell over. Probably a heart attack.'

She rushed forward and threw herself down, face close to his, checking throat and wrists for pulse.

'You're right, the bastard's dead.'

She jumped up. I expected tears and distress.

Instead her face changed from shock to delight. She threw arms round me in a great happy hug.

'Thank God. We're free.'

I pushed her away.

'What the fuck are you talking about?'

'I've been waiting for someone to kill him for years. I don't know how you did it but thanks a million billion. I'm now the boss. I take over.'

'How?'

'I know most of his secrets. I know every supplier and customer and where most of the cash is. Now it's all mine and so is his organisation. We'll run it together.'

'I can't do that.'

Her elegant happy face switched in an instance from beautiful to ugly. Her large liquid eyes became hard and narrowed with suspicion.

'You'll do what I say without question or argument. I'm the boss now and the job you came here for is finished. So you're finished with whoever sent you. From this moment you work for me and no one else. Understand?'

'No. I don't understand.'

'I think you're the woman who spent time asking questions in Nice and Paris. You're the woman who killed his men in Nice and Paris. You came here to stalk and kill my husband. Now you've done it you're under my control. You do as I say or my boys will take you for a special swim.'

She strolled across the room and sat on the double divan. With that graceful up-and-back sweep of her hands she lifted and dropped her mane of hair in a flowing wave across her shoulders.

'Now come and sit here and we'll decide what to do with him.'

Instead I crouched by the body and said, 'Surely we'd better check he's really dead then call the coroner.'

'Of course he's dead. Come and sit here.'

I ran my hand across The Bishop's cold skin and felt his neck.

'There's a pulse,' I cried. 'Come and feel.'

In a second her face crumbled from haughty aggression to absolute terror.

'Are you sure?'

'Come and feel for yourself.'

She dropped to hands and knees and crawled forward, hunched and fearful.

'Come and feel. We must call someone, a doctor or your Chinaman.'

'No,' she whispered. I want him dead. Can you finish him off for me? Please do it. For me. Finish him off.'

'You check that he's alive first.'

She reached with a trembling hand.

I drew my tuning fork along her arm.

Another gasp, another death.

Pulling her body across I laid it alongside The Bishop and arranged them with arms crossed over chests. I stood back to admire my handiwork.

A good looking couple joined in death. Quite medieval. Although the art of it may be lost on whoever eventually finds them.

By chance her dress and mine were almost identical colours but she also sported a large blue scarf. I took it and wrapped the flow of material over my hair, allowing several tresses to float free. Unless closely examined we looked so alike – flowing blond hair, trim figures – I had good chance of getting out of the place without having to kill anyone else.

I took her key, locked the door and floated down the stairs, waving Chinaman away. Opening the door myself I saw my Chessman waiting by the car.

'Finished for the day?' he laughed.

'Just started,' I said. 'I have to look after you next.'

He opened the rear door and I settled in.

'Off to my place for our own private fun, then,' he said.

'I'm looking forward to it,'

He gave thumbs up at the gate guards waving us through. 'They think you're the Boss's wife.'

'What luck. I don't want to waste time.'

'Me neither.'

'But first can you take me to the rail station? I have some things there to collect.'

'Sure. It's near my pad.'

He pulled into a shaded space at the edge of the car park.

Before he could speak I gave the back of his neck the tuning fork treatment, catching him as he slumped forward.

I arranged him with his head laid back as though bored and dozing, hurried to the station luggage lockers and retrieved my suitcase and disappeared into the ladies restroom.

Ten minutes later, anyone who earlier saw that gossamer beauty floating through the concourse would not connect her to the dumpy middle-aged woman in plain skirt and blouse clumping along on heavy low heeled shoes and old-fashioned spectacles.

On the train to Italy she kept herself to herself, reading a succession of religious magazines with great concentration.

Chapter 45

I always like Italy.

Unless a woman is young and beautiful it is a great place to pass un-noticed. The men watch only big backsides and bosoms, ignoring any poor girl who doesn't sashay past with rolling hips.

So Miss Religious booked into a backstreet hotel and went shopping. Back at the hotel she changed personality to successful travel writer and walked out through an empty lobby.

She went to another town and stayed two nights, visiting historic churches and buildings for her current book before changing city by bus to re-emerge as Eleanor for a restful week in a luxury hotel.

There followed two months of weaving around the world from country to country, entering by one airport and leaving by another or crossing borders by train or bus.

Along the way I switched between Eleanor and travel writer several times. In some cities Eleanor worked a few days in a of high class brothel or as a call girl for a little light relief and relaxation.

When the travel writer reached her secluded little house among the trees I found a note from my agent saying Publisher loved my previous books and asked for more as soon as possible.

I seem to have done well in my two chosen careers because my anonymous employers pinged congratulations to my Cloud Mail-Box and dropped two million extra dollars into my hidden bank account.

I told my agent I had three books to complete and asked my employers for time to rest before travelling again. And, for something different to do, volunteered to work in a nearby home for disadvantaged children.

I enjoy being with the nuns and think that if you are lucky enough to have a rewarding productive life yourself, you should give something back to others less well off.

Chapter 46

I stayed happy and secure in my secluded woodlands house for almost six months, helping the nuns and disadvantaged children two or three days a week.

Work in completing and editing my three travel books kept me busy and gave good excuse to avoid contact with neighbours.

Shortly after publication of the third book my Cloud Mail-Box pinged its first coded message for some time.

Go to the Turks and Caicos and await instructions.